'I will do whatever it takes, Andreas! Anything to make Lilly's life more secure.'

'Anything…?' He leaned back against the counter and surveyed her lazily. 'Somehow I don't think a nun's habit would suit you, Carrie. Maybe you need to rethink that.'

'Joke all you want.' Carrie tipped her head up defiantly. 'But I am prepared to put Lilly first. Whereas you—at the end of the day it's still going to be your staff who tuck Lilly into bed, while you're tied up with the business.'

Andreas held her gaze. 'Not if I take a wife.'

Kathryn Ross was born in Zambia, where her parents happened to live at that time. Educated in Ireland and England, she now lives in a village near Blackpool, Lancashire. Kathryn is a professional beauty therapist, but writing is her first love. As a child she wrote adventure stories, and at thirteen was editor of her school magazine. Happily, ten writing years later, DESIGNED WITH LOVE was accepted by Mills & Boon®. A romantic Sagittarian, she loves travelling to exotic locations.

Recent titles by the same author:

KEPT BY HER GREEK BOSS
THE ITALIAN'S UNWILLING WIFE

THE MEDITERRANEAN'S WIFE BY CONTRACT

BY

KATHRYN ROSS

MILLS & BOON®

Pure reading pleasure™

First published in Great Britain 2009
Harlequin Mills & Boon Limited,
Eton House, 18-24 Paradise Road, Richmond, Surrey TW9 1SR

ISBN: 978 0 263 20810 8

Set in Times Roman 10¼ on 11½ pt
07-0709-55631

Printed and bound in Great Britain
by CPI Antony Rowe, Chippenham, Wiltshire

THE
MEDITERRANEAN'S
WIFE BY CONTRACT

CHAPTER ONE

A BLIND date wasn't Carrie's idea of fun. But since day two of their holiday together when Jo had met Theo she had been determinedly insisting that Carrie just had to meet his handsome older brother.

'Honestly, the moment you see him you'll know what I mean,' Jo had told her seriously. 'If I wasn't head over heels about Theo I'd be interested in him myself. Andreas is absolutely gorgeous, and a really nice guy.'

'Jo, if you are doing this because you don't want me to be left alone then you really don't need to worry. After the last few months working for my degree I'm perfectly happy to be left to do some serious relaxing, soaking up the sun and—'

'Yes, I know, you said all that—but you really need to meet him, Carrie. He's a real Greek Adonis—honestly. Just humour me; meet Andreas once for a few hours one evening. We'll make it a foursome—how's that? We'll have pre-dinner drinks together at that lovely little taverna on the waterside. And if you are hitting it off you can stay and we'll have dinner together— if you're not, you can tell him you've already eaten and leave. But you will like him—honestly.'

On day four of the holiday in a moment of weakness Carrie had agreed. Now here she was sitting at a table by herself feeling more than a little apprehensive. Jo and her new boyfriend Theo had been delayed. And heaven alone knew where Andreas was. Possibly dragging his heels if Theo had strong-armed him as heavily as Jo had her.

She should never have agreed to this, Carrie thought with embarrassment.

At least the waterside taverna was an idyllic place to wait.

The sun was setting in a glorious shade of crimson, turning the sea a flame red, and giving a spectacular end to another long hot day on the small Greek island of Pyrena.

Carrie breathed in the warm evening air, fragrant with jasmine and the salt of the sea, and relaxed. With a bit of luck Theo's brother wouldn't turn up and Carrie could make a hasty escape and leave Jo and Theo to enjoy a romantic evening together. They needed to make the most of their time, because in another ten days the holiday would be over and she and Jo would be heading back to London. Jo would be devastated to leave—Carrie had never seen her so captivated by a guy. It was completely out of character. And Theo seemed to feel exactly the same way. They had just clicked immediately and now, even though they'd only known each other a few days, it was as if they had always been together.

Was that true love? Carrie wondered.

Darkness was stealing over the landscape and a waiter was lighting some candles on the tables nearby ready for the evening ahead. As yet the place was quiet, just one other couple dining at a table tucked away in a far corner. She glanced at her watch. Jo was now ten minutes late. Maybe if she wasn't here in another ten Carrie could sneak away—because the more she thought about it, the more she didn't want to be here. Jo and Theo needed to be alone, not wasting precious time needlessly matchmaking! Why couldn't they understand that she was happy on her own reading her book? She didn't want to meet anyone.

'Are you waiting for someone?'

The question made Carrie look up and shock sizzled its way through her entire body.

If this was Andreas, then Jo hadn't been exaggerating! He

was absolutely gorgeous—in fact he was probably the most handsome man Carrie had ever set eyes on in her life.

He was tall yet powerfully built and he was wearing an expensive-looking dark suit with casual flare that only continental men seemed to achieve so effortlessly. A crisp blue shirt was open at the strong column of his neck. His thick dark hair was cut short accentuating chiselled features and a strong jaw. But it was his eyes that held her spellbound, they were the colour of dark molasses, intense, almost arrogant in their assessment of her.

Aware that he was waiting for a reply she tried to gather herself together with some difficulty. 'Yes…some friends—'

'You must be Carrie?'

She nodded. Was it her imagination, she wondered, or was the air electrically charged between them? Their eyes seemed to hold for a fraction too long before his gaze swept over her in a bold unconcealed scrutiny of her appearance from her long blonde hair and sweetheart-shaped face, down over the curves of her figure in the bright blue summer dress.

And shockingly Carrie felt a thrust of sensual heat stir deep inside her at that slow, sexy deliberation.

'Andreas Stillanos.' He held out his hand and she took it, aware that as their skin touched she felt the zing of attraction deepen. She liked the strong firm touch of his skin against hers. She liked everything about him.

This was crazy, she thought with a mounting sense of panic. A man had never had this effect on her before; so, OK, he was good-looking—so what? She didn't know him—how could she feel so intensely…*turned on* just by the way he was looking at her?

But the simple truth was that she did—there was something almost raw and primitive about it. Carrie couldn't explain it; all she knew was that it was scaring her to death! She was a sensible person, grounded—realistic—this was a kind of madness that she didn't want.

She watched as Andreas pulled out the chair opposite her and sat down.

For a moment there was silence, filled only with the relentless sizzle of the tide as it brushed over the stony beach beside them, a sound that seemed to echo the sensations inside her body.

'Jo and Theo have been delayed,' she told him, trying hard to pull herself together.

'Yes, so I gathered.' His lips curved in an amused smile.

She supposed she had stated the obvious! Carrie tried to compose herself, tried to think of something else to say, but as their eyes held she found the task increasingly difficult.

A waiter appeared next to them and Andreas spoke to him in Greek. The sound was deep and sexy and Carrie was even further entranced.

'Can I get you another drink, Carrie?' He switched effortlessly to perfect English again and looked over at her.

'No, I'm fine, thank you.' Carrie indicated her glass of wine that was almost full.

They were left alone again.

'I think the delay is something to do with Theo's dive shop,' Carrie continued, trying to stay focused on anything except the feelings he was generating inside her. 'Apparently he stayed open later than usual to accommodate some customers who are going home to England tomorrow.'

Andreas regarded her sardonically. 'Personally, I think the delay is more to do with throwing us together on our own for a while.'

That thought hadn't occurred to her until he suggested it so bluntly and Carrie felt a surge of red-hot embarrassment. 'I don't think so!' But even as she rejected the idea she wondered if it were true—were Jo and Theo deliberately late? Honestly, it was too mortifying!

'Don't you?' He seemed to be watching her with very close attention, and she knew that even though they were sitting in the semi-darkness of the star-lit evening he could see that she was blushing.

The knowledge and the way he was watching her made her flush even more. 'Well, Jo rang me to apologise for their delay and she sounded genuinely agitated. She always likes to be on time.'

'So you haven't felt obligated to meet me, then?' he asked with a mocking lift of one eyebrow. 'Because to be honest Theo hasn't stopped going on about you for the last few days.'

'And you found yourself agreeing to this evening's arrangements just to get some peace?' Carrie wanted the ground to open up and swallow her. 'It's OK; I have to admit to a similar situation. Jo has been going on rather a lot about you too. I think she feels guilty about leaving me—but I keep telling her I'm perfectly happy.'

'They've fallen in love and now they think that the whole world needs to follow suit,' Andreas said wryly.

The waiter arrived with his drink and Carrie had never been so very glad of an interruption. It was obvious from his derisive words that Andreas had wanted this blind date even less than she had! And she noticed he'd ordered a Greek coffee—hardly a pre-dinner drink. He wasn't even pretending that he might stay.

As they were left alone again he glanced up and their eyes met. 'Unfortunately I have a business meeting back in Athens early tomorrow. So I can't stay long.'

'Well—I can't stay long either.' Carrie rallied herself, her pride rising to her defence. 'I was just thinking before you arrived that we should get this over with as quickly as possible. Jo and Theo should be making each moment count, having a nice romantic time on their own.'

'Yes, I suppose they should.' Andreas looked over at her with a teasing gleam in the darkness of his eyes. 'But I wouldn't worry too much. I'm sure their time has been put to some good use.'

Meaning what, Carrie wondered, as opposed to their time?

'So how are you enjoying your holiday on Pyrena?' he asked as he sat back into his chair.

Now he was trying to make polite conversation. This was excruciating.

For her friend's sake she forced herself to smile and answer courteously. 'I'm having a lovely time, thank you. It's a beautiful island.'

'Have you been out to see the coral reef yet?'

Carrie shook her head. 'Theo and Jo invited me to go out there with them yesterday but I don't dive.'

'You could snorkel.'

'I'm not a strong swimmer and I don't like to be out of my depth.'

'You just need someone experienced alongside. You should try it—it really is beautiful out there.' His mobile rang and he reached to answer it immediately. 'Excuse me Carrie,' he said politely as he flicked it open.

She listened as he spoke in Greek, his voice crisp and businesslike, and his expression serious.

He was far too attractive, Carrie thought as she allowed her eyes to drift over him. Dangerously so.

She wondered what it would be like to feel those sensual lips exploring hers, those hands touching her skin.

He hung up and glanced over at her again. 'Sorry about that—business, I'm afraid.'

'That's OK.' Annoyed by her thoughts, she looked away from him and lifted her glass of wine. What on earth was the matter with her? Andreas couldn't have made it clearer that he was uncomfortable with this situation and wasn't interested in her and yet here she was daydreaming about kissing him! 'You know, if you need to go don't let me detain you. I'll pass on your apologies to Theo and Jo.'

'I don't think you'll need to. They're here.'

Carrie followed his glance out towards the road and saw Theo climbing out of his black sports car, closely followed by Jo. She noticed the way Theo waited for her by the pavement, reached out and took her hand.

There was something very touching about the moment, about the way Jo looked up at him.

'Somehow they seem right together, don't they?' Carrie didn't realize she had spoken aloud until Andreas answered her.

'Yes. I think this is serious.'

Carrie glanced over at him, his words resonating inside her. He was right.

So what was going to happen at the end of the holiday when it was time for Jo to go home? Her friend deserved happiness so much, Carrie thought as she turned her attention back towards them. She'd been through so much in her life—Carrie knew exactly how tough she'd had it because they'd grown up together in the same foster home. She knew that Jo pretended to be tough but had a heart as kind and as soft as you could get.

As they approached Carrie thought her friend had never looked lovelier. She was wearing a black fitted dress that did great things for her slender figure, and her skin was glowing, her long blonde curls softly tousled around her face. 'I'm so sorry we're late,' she murmured, looking from one to the other of them searchingly.

'It was entirely my fault.' Theo cut in as he reached to kiss Carrie on both cheeks. 'Nice to see you again, Carrie, and I'm really sorry, time just ran away with us. But we knew you two would be hitting it off.'

Carrie wished she hadn't met Andreas's eyes across the table just at that moment.

He looked lazily amused, which irritated Carrie considerably.

'Don't worry about it,' he said nonchalantly as he got to his feet to greet them. 'Carrie and I have enjoyed meeting.'

'Oh, good!' Jo looked at Carrie with an 'I told you so' glint in her eyes and Carrie tried her utmost to look unfazed. Was Jo so blinded by love that she failed to notice Andreas's obvious reluctance to be here?

'So, is everything OK?' Jo asked in an undertone as she took the seat beside her.

'Absolutely.' Carrie was distracted for a moment as she

watched Andreas greet his younger brother. She noticed how alike they were, both tall and dark, but Theo's features were open, pleasant, less challenging than Andreas's, who had a powerful, hard intensity about his good looks.

It was immediately apparent that the men were not just brothers, but that they were also good friends. They talked together for a moment about Theo's business, Theo asking Andreas's opinion on some new equipment that he wanted.

'They would talk for ever about business.' Jo grinned at Carrie.

'Hey, I need all the advice I can get,' Theo cut in good-naturedly. 'Especially from a brother who has a brilliant mind for business—I don't know what I'd do without him.'

'You'd do very well, Theo. Your business is flourishing,' Andreas told him staunchly.

'Not without your help.' Theo glanced around for the waiter. 'Shall we grab some menus? I don't know about everyone else but I am very hungry.'

'Unfortunately I'm not going to be able to stay.' Andreas glanced at his watch. 'I have to head off to Athens—I have a meeting early tomorrow.'

'Oh, no! But surely you can stay a little longer?' Jo couldn't contain her disappointment.

'Afraid not.' Andreas glanced over at Carrie. 'But it has been really lovely meeting you, Carrie.'

The urbane civility of the words made Carrie cringe. 'Yes—likewise.' She smiled politely back at him.

Their eyes held for a moment.

Andreas noticed how she tilted her head up, an almost re-bellious fiery light in her eyes. Obviously she'd been as uncom-fortable with this situation as he had.

She was stunningly beautiful—Theo hadn't been embellish-ing. But there was also an unusual fragility about her, and a reserve that fascinated him. Most young women flirted openly with him, but she hadn't even tried to capture his interest, there had been no coy smiles, or false joviality. Just that proud tilt of her head as she looked across at him and when she smiled—really smiled, not in that polite way she was now—it blew him away.

But he didn't have time for such things, he reminded himself firmly. He was in the midst of difficult business negotiations and now was not a good time for a dalliance. Besides, this situation could be a minefield. Theo was deeply involved with Carrie's best friend and by contrast Andreas wasn't looking for anything serious and never would be, so it was probably best to steer clear of muddying these waters.

'I'll leave you to enjoy your evening.' He rose smoothly to his feet.

'Damn!' Jo muttered the word angrily under her breath as they watched him walk away. 'I'm so sorry, Carrie... I really thought you two would hit it off!'

'We did. We enjoyed a very pleasant drink together,' Carrie hastily reassured her friend. 'Don't waste your time worrying about it!'

'Andreas really is in the middle of a most gruelling takeover deal,' Theo inserted quickly. 'He's just sold his publishing house and now he's buying out shares in a newspaper company—playing for very high stakes. If his meeting is early in the morning he will have to take the late ferry to Athens tonight and stay at his apartment there.'

'Theo, you don't need to explain.' Carrie was discomfited by how upset they both were and also touched by their staunch regard of her feelings. 'Andreas and I had a lovely time chatting as we waited for you. I thoroughly enjoyed his company. But we both agreed that you two need time on your own, and to be honest I'm really glad of the opportunity to go back to the apartment and have an early night.'

'You are not going anywhere!' Jo said with a raised eyebrow. 'You are having dinner with us—we insist!'

'But honestly, Jo—'

'I wouldn't argue if I were you,' Theo told her with a grin. 'Because you won't win.'

CHAPTER TWO

CARRIE was sipping water as she lounged on the sunbed reading her book. This was quite blissful, she thought as she stretched lazily to put her glass down. But in a moment she was going to have to work up the energy to move into the shade.

London felt like another planet away. There were only a few people around the apartment-complex pool—and the tranquillity of the setting amidst green manicured gardens was very relaxing.

Jo had just left to go and have a coffee with Theo at the dive shop. She'd asked Carrie to accompany her but after the embarrassment of meeting Andreas last night she definitely preferred to be alone. That had to be the most uncomfortable half hour of her life.

However, he had been incredibly good-looking. For a second she remembered the dark, searing intensity of his eyes, remembered the craziness of her thoughts—the weird feelings of longing. She was twenty-two years of age and no man had ever stirred that kind of reaction in her before.

In fact, men had chased her, flirted with her, even kissed her and hadn't awoken that kind of response. She'd started to wonder if perhaps she didn't have it in her to feel passion, because she always thought things through—analysed relationships to the utmost degree.

Jo had told her she had a trust problem when it came to men, and she knew deep down that her friend was probably right, that it was probably because her father had walked out on her when she'd been young. She'd even started to accept that about herself—accept the fact that maybe she would never allow herself to let go and just be swept away by emotions. And yet last night all Andreas had done was look at her and she had felt more alive—more turned on—than she ever had before!

Too much sun combined with holiday madness, she told herself swiftly as she switched her attention back to her book. Andreas wasn't even interested in her—and she wasn't interested in him!

Her phone rang and she quickly reached to answer it before it could disturb the peace and quiet of the afternoon. She couldn't see whose name was flashing on the dial but she guessed it would be Jo ringing to see if she would change her mind and join them.

'Hi, Jo—will you stop fussing? I'm by the pool doing nothing and loving every minute,' she told her breezily.

'Well, I'm glad to hear it.' The amused male voice sent so many disconcerting waves of shock rushing through her that she almost dropped the phone. She knew instantly who it was; there was no mistaking that deeply sensual almost lazy intonation. And it was so weird hearing his voice after she'd just been thinking about him. As if dark forces had conjured him up!

Trying desperately to dispel the ridiculous thoughts, she sat up on the sunbed, her book falling to the ground, and said the first thing that came into her head. 'Andreas, where on earth did you get my phone number?'

'Well, now, you can have two guesses,' he replied teasingly, 'but if you'd like a hint, I've just seen Theo at the shop. He wanted some advice on this equipment he's buying—'

'And you allowed him to talk you into calling me! Andreas, I know you think a lot of your brother, but this goes beyond the line of duty—'

'Hey, can I just stop you right there?' he cut across her firmly. 'For once Theo didn't even mention you—I asked him for your number.'

There was a moment's silence and Carrie wondered if she had misheard him. 'Why did you do that?'

'Because I have some free time this afternoon, and I wondered if you'd like to go out to the coral reef with me.'

The invitation was deeply tempting but she forced herself to take a deep breath and think sensibly. 'Thank you, I appreciate the kind offer, but I'm busy—'

'I thought you just said you were doing nothing?' He sounded even more amused now.

'Yes, I'm busy doing nothing and loving it.'

'So come and be energetic with me and you'll love it even more.'

The teasing husky words made her adrenalin surge wildly.

'I'll pick you up in about ten minutes.'

'Ten minutes! I thought you were in Athens this morning!' Her voice rose slightly.

'I was, for an early breakfast meeting. That finished early enough for me to catch the ferry over, so now I'm just down the road from your hotel—I told you, I've been out to see Theo.'

'Andreas, I won't be ready—'

'Then I'll wait—but not for long, so get a move on.'

The phone went dead and Carrie held it away from her ear and glared at it as if it were a living entity.

How dared he take her acceptance for granted? Did he think that just because her friend had been so keen to set her up with him that she was some kind of sad charity case? Well, she would soon put him right about that! She wasn't going to go out with him! He would arrive and she would still be lying here reading her book.

Carrie picked it up and adjusted her floppy hat down over her eyes and tried to focus back on the page.

But all she could think about was Andreas. Why had he

suddenly phoned her like this? She really had thought she would never hear from him again.

Should she swallow her pride and go out with him? She had to admit she was more than a little curious about the feelings he had stirred within her last night—had it just been some flight of fancy on her behalf?

She glared at the printed page, hating herself for weakening. Andreas had made it abundantly clear he wasn't interested in her last night—so this was probably some kind of sop to his brother's feelings, because Theo had been as upset as Jo when he'd walked out.

She glanced up over the pages of her book as she heard a car pulling up outside. A few moments later she saw Andreas strolling in through the front gates of the property. He looked magnificent. There was no other word for it. His clothes were casual, a white linen shirt and sand-coloured trousers, yet he looked incredibly sophisticated and stylish—or was that simply the air of confidence that he wore like a well fitting cape?

Carrie immediately wished she'd rushed inside to get changed. Not that she had many stylish clothes with her. The dress she'd worn last night was it—everything else was shorts, tee shirts and jeans. But it was too late to even think about that now, she realized with a rapidly beating heart as he glanced over and caught her eye.

'Ah, there you are.' He cut away from the path and walked across the grass towards her and she noticed the interested glances he received from some attractive young women nearby.

She tried to pretend that she was engrossed in her book, only nonchalantly glancing up as he reached her side. She wasn't going to give him the satisfaction of knowing that she too found it hard to take her eyes off him.

He seemed to tower over her, and that combined with the fact that she was only wearing a bikini made her feel suddenly extremely self-conscious.

She sat up a little straighter on the bed and then drew her

knees up in an attempt to shield her body from his eyes. But she realized that wasn't working as his gaze just moved over her long legs with swift male appraisal.

'I don't know what you are doing here, Andreas,' she murmured nervously.

'Don't you…?' His lips curved in a smile that made her heart rate start to increase. Then he took a chair from a nearby table and sat down beside her. 'I thought I told you when we spoke on the phone.'

'And I thought we'd dealt with this situation last night. Theo and Jo mean well,' she continued briskly, 'but we shouldn't feel obliged to spend time together just to please them.'

'Is that what you think this is?' One dark eyebrow lifted. 'I never do anything I don't want to do, Carrie…I can assure you of that.'

'Well, you turned up last night!' she reminded him swiftly.

'Yes, out of curiosity.' He smiled. 'You're right when you say that I think a lot of my brother—but dating to please him…?' He looked at her wryly and shook his head. 'That was never going to happen.'

'Yes, well, I feel exactly the same where Jo is concerned, so let's just leave it like that.' She flicked her chin up stubbornly.

'Good, I'm glad you feel the same—because it means we can just be friends, doesn't it?'

She liked the way he held her eyes as he said those words. Could a woman ever just be a friend with someone who looked like him? Carrie wondered.

'I don't do serious relationships anyway,' he added gently. 'I don't want complications, nor have I got time for them, especially at the moment.'

'Neither have I.' She angled her chin up even further. 'I'm on holiday to relax after working extremely hard for exams. And in nine days' time I start a new job in the city.'

'So a bit of light-hearted fun is in order all round.'

She wanted to ask him what kind of fun he was talking

about, but she didn't dare voice that question because it seemed far too dangerous.

'So, the bottom line is that you're at a loose end this afternoon?' she said instead.

He laughed at that. 'Maybe it is.'

'Well, I'll have to check my appointments diary.' She nodded. 'Because I'm *really* busy…'

He liked the playful gleam in her blue eyes.

'Yes, I can see that.' His glance moved towards the book that she was still holding in her hands and he reached out and took it from her. At first she thought he was taking it away, but he simply turned it around and handed it back and she realized she'd been holding it upside down!

She flushed with embarrassment. 'I dropped it a few moments ago.'

He nodded. 'It's obviously riveting.'

'It is…but I suppose I could tear myself away from it for a few hours. I'm not so sure about snorkelling at the reef, though…as I told you last night I am not a strong swimmer.'

'Well…we'll sail out there, assess your skills and take it from there. How's that?'

'Sounds OK.'

He nodded. 'And if you don't want to swim or snorkel you can watch the boat whilst I dive. You don't have to do anything you don't want to do.'

'Oh, right, so I'm just the lookout for sharks now, am I?'

'No, I'll promote you. You can be the bar manager,' he amended.

'Gee, thanks.' She laughed. 'Just give me a minute to go inside and change.'

'You're fine the way you are.' She was wearing a very sexy red bikini that showed off her incredible figure to perfection: high pert breasts, a narrow waist, and slender hips. 'Just throw on your shorts and T-shirt.' He picked them up from the bottom of her sunbed and tossed them up at her.

She caught them instinctively. 'But my money is in the apartment safe so I need to go back inside anyway.'

'You don't need money.' He watched as she took off her sunhat and her hair tumbled around her shoulders and down to her waist in a golden silky wave.

She was so beautiful that he found it difficult to look away. He noticed how her ribs protruded as she stretched upwards to put her T-shirt on and how flat her stomach was and he longed suddenly to reach out and touch her, slide his hands over the satin perfection of her skin. As she stood up from the bed and pulled her shorts on she flicked a glance over at him.

It was a look that was both vulnerable yet filled with an answering fire. The same look she had thrown him last night. It intrigued him...

Not many women had that effect on him, and there had been no shortage of beautiful women in his life over the years. Mostly he hadn't had to pursue any with too much rigour; they'd fallen into his bed with the greatest of ease—and he'd enjoyed them, whilst being as honest as he could about the fact that he had no intention of committing to a real relationship. The strange thing was that the more elusive he was, the more interested they became. But it wasn't a game with him—he really didn't want to get himself entwined in a serious relationship. He'd been there and wouldn't return.

Presently there were no women in his life—he'd cleared the decks because he needed all his time and concentration for the intricate negotiations of the takeover deal. Ditching his social life for these last few weeks hadn't cost him a second thought. He was completely focused on the deal.

Or rather he had been until this morning when during a meeting of the board he had suddenly been distracted by thoughts of Carrie.

He hadn't been able to get her out of his head all night either. That almost defiant way she'd looked at him with clear sky-blue eyes. The way her skin flushed so easily, and vulnerability slipped in. She was a bewitching mix of innocence laced with provoking passion and despite telling himself to stay away he just couldn't.

Right now he should have been in a meeting with his accountants, not here with her. But, he reasoned, he deserved an afternoon off anyway. They would keep things light and tomorrow he would regain his complete focus on business.

Andreas had recommended that she kept her shirt on to protect her delicate fair skin from burning whilst snorkelling, but all he wore were his trunks. She watched from the back of the boat as he dived cleanly into the calm turquoise water. He looked like an Olympic athlete, she thought admiringly; his body was perfectly honed, his skin gleaming a rich honey gold. He disappeared for a moment beneath the satin surface of the sea and then resurfaced. 'Right, your turn.'

'Very funny. I can't dive like that!'

He grinned. 'Go down onto the platform and slide in. Don't worry—I'll catch you if you have any difficulty.'

Carrie didn't know which made her heart race faster: the thought of him putting his arms around her or the vast depths of the ocean.

'Come on, it's lovely once you're in,' he coaxed.

Taking a deep breath, she went down the ladder onto the back platform and then allowed herself to slide in. The water felt surprisingly icy and she gasped.

'Gosh! It's cold.'

He laughed and swam over so that he was next to her. 'It's not cold, you're just hot.' He added teasingly, 'In more ways than one.'

It was amazing—even in the cool water she could feel the heat of his gaze licking through her. He was so very close; she could see the gold flecks in the darkness of his eyes, noticed how thick and dark his eyelashes were, how sensual and inviting the arrogant curve of his lips.

She wanted to reach out and touch him. Instead she forced herself to swim away. 'So where is the reef?'

'A little further out.' He picked up the masks he'd left on the platform and headed after her.

Carrie didn't think she would ever forget being alone with Andreas that afternoon, surrounded by nothing but the vastness of the sea. The water was so tranquil and clear, and, when her skin became accustomed to it, quite warm. Andreas showed her how to use the snorkelling equipment and stayed close until she was feeling more confident. And by then she was enraptured by the secret world beneath them.

The reef was spectacular, a giant living city of swaying tentacles and flower shapes that moved with a swirl of its colourful fish inhabitants.

She loved every minute of it and was disappointed when Andreas told her it was time to head back to the boat.

'That was fabulous.' She smiled happily up at him as he climbed on the platform and reached to help her out of the water.

'You're glad you did it, then?'

'Really glad. I wouldn't have missed it for the world.'

'You certainly looked at home. In fact, you looked like a mermaid with your hair streaming behind you as you swam.'

She laughed. 'Well, unless this T-shirt dries out quickly I'm going to look like a bedraggled fish out of water on the way home.'

'You can borrow a shirt of mine to put on.' He led the way up onto the deck. 'Although I have to say that the bedraggled look also suits you.'

Distracted by his gentle flirting, she lost her footing as she stepped down onto the polished floor.

Immediately he caught her and for the briefest moment she was held close against the powerful lines of his wet body.

Then he released her.

'Sorry about that. I just slipped.' She tried to sound nonchalant, and smile at him, but the contact had knocked all the breath from her body, and the curl of dangerous excitement deep inside her was still there.

Disconcerted, she looked away. 'I suppose we should head back to the island now.'

'Yes, I guess so. I have work to get back to.' His glance moved over her, he hadn't been lying when he'd told her that she looked good. Her wet hair was slicked back from her face revealing her perfect skin, her high cheekbones.

His gaze moved lower, noticing how the wet shirt was moulded to the shapely curves of her body and how taut and firm her body was.

He wanted to peel the shirt off her and unfasten the bikini, let his mouth and his tongue explore her warm, wet curves.

His eyes moved upwards and connected with hers and suddenly naked hunger burned like a blue flame between them. Carrie felt a thrill of need kick inside and take over her desire so intense it made her feel powerless.

How was this happening to her? she wondered in panic. How could he make her want him so desperately with just the slightest touch, and one look?

She made to turn away but he caught hold of her hand and pulled her back.

The next moment she was in his arms and his mouth was on hers, possessing her with an almost ruthless intent.

No one had ever kissed her with such total demanding control and she hesitated for a moment as shock pounded through her, and then pleasure detonated inside her. It felt so good, as if he were reaching inside her, drawing out the secrets of her soul...

She kissed him back, her arms sliding up and around his neck, aware that at the same time his hands were moving beneath her wet shirt, stroking up over her.

The sensation of pleasure was so exquisitely irresistible that she ached for more, ached to be rid of all the clothes and have no barrier between them. All she could think about was how much she wanted him—and how she could intensify the enjoy-ment—how she never wanted him to let her go.

'I wanted to do this from the moment I saw you again this

afternoon.' He murmured the words against her ear as his hand slid down to stroke over her bikini-clad bottom, pulling her in against the hard arousal of his body.

'And I thought you just wanted to be friends.'

'Well, I want that too… I want everything…' he murmured, stroking his hand along the smooth curves of her hips. 'Everything you want to give…' His fingers teased across over her thighs and then swept higher to the soft core of her through the material of her costume. 'I'm greedy like that.'

Carrie found herself gasping with pleasure as his lips took control of hers again. She felt greedy too…and impatient, and where lovemaking was concerned these were emotions she'd never had to deal with before.

She tried to tell herself she didn't know this man, that she should be cautious because this was nothing more than a holiday fling. Did she really want her first time to be just a casual encounter? But her body was fighting the thoughts, pushing them away with almost mocking disregard so that her reasoning was lost like a whisper in a hurricane.

'Maybe we should go inside, make ourselves more comfortable,' he suggested as his fingers stroked ever more tantalizingly over her.

She couldn't answer him, couldn't formulate any words. His lips moved down over the column of her neck with butterfly kisses and she held him closer. He pressed against her, parting her legs, and suddenly she realized he was responding to her urgency and if she didn't say anything he would just take her right here, right now…

Momentary panic zinged through her as she felt how powerful his body was against hers and she froze. Immediately he pulled back.

'What is it?' His voice was distracted as he traced his hands up over her narrow waist and ribcage. Then he looked into her eyes… And for just a fleeting second he saw her vulnerability.

'You have done this before…haven't you?'

It was almost a throwaway question, but when she didn't answer shocked realization flooded through him closely followed by the knowledge that maybe he'd suspected her innocence all along… Yes…when he thought about the delightful way she blushed so easily, her way of avoiding his gaze sometimes, and of course the vulnerable gleam in those beautiful eyes. Even the hesitant way she'd first met the demands of his kiss.

Deep down he'd known…

'You're a virgin.' It was more statement than question. Then he said something in Greek softly under his breath as he pulled her shirt down to cover her body again.

'Andreas?' She looked up at him questioningly, and as she saw him moving back from her it was as if icy cold water were suddenly flooding through her veins.

'Carrie…this…changes things.' He said the words slowly as he tried to get his brain to operate without the almost violent intervention of the desire he still felt for her.

She frowned. She didn't want this conversation; all she wanted was for him to take her back into his arms. 'Does it?'

'Of course it does!' He raked a hand through the darkness of his hair. 'You're young and beautiful, and obviously a virgin by choice.'

'Well…yes…' She frowned, not understanding where he was going with the conversation.

'Which means you don't do casual relationships—and that's all I have to offer.'

He watched how her skin coloured. 'Carrie, I don't want to hurt you,' he added gently.

'No, of course not…and you're right, this would be a bad mistake!' Her voice came out in a rush as reality swooped in. She couldn't believe what she had so nearly done! Obviously this would be nothing more than casual sex. Something she had always avoided.

Hell—from as far back as she could remember she'd always

promised herself that she would be in control of relationships. She'd witnessed at first hand the devastating consequences of loving the wrong person.

She swallowed hard as she looked over at him, her pride stinging. 'But I'd no intention of going further—I was just enjoying a bit of light-hearted fooling around.'

'Were you now?' His voice held amusement and she felt her skin scorch with sudden wild heat as she remembered how eagerly she had returned his advances.

'I don't know what I was thinking,' she admitted.

'Well…I know what I was thinking.' His voice was husky, his eyes on her lips. He reached out and stroked a stray strand of her hair back from her face.

'Don't, Andreas.' She flinched away from him. 'Let's just put this down to a little bit of madness, and forget it, OK.'

Andreas frowned. He didn't want to forget it—but nor could he proceed…not now…not with any conscience.

'Anyway, we said we'd head back to land now, didn't we?' she said quickly.

'Yes, dry land and sanity.' He turned away from her and headed up to the bridge. She was off limits, he told himself firmly. And that was the end of it.

Carrie picked up one of the towels that Andreas had left out for her earlier and wrapped it around her slender figure. She was trembling with cold—yet the sun was blazing down on her. It was the strangest feeling.

CHAPTER THREE

CARRIE was sure there would be a strained silence between them in the car on the way home, except that as soon as Andreas switched on his phone and put it into hands-free mode it kept ringing. He took one call after another as he drove slowly back along the coast road.

Carrie couldn't understand a word he was saying, but it was obviously all to do with business because he dealt with each call in the same serious, crisply concise voice.

'My apologies, Carrie. I employ a team of accountants and yet they still need me to hold their hands,' he muttered in annoyance as he started to say something to her and the phone rang again.

'That's OK.' She shrugged and looked away from him. In truth she was glad. She couldn't wait to get away from him, pretend that this afternoon hadn't happened.

He finished his call just as the gates to her apartment complex loomed and as soon as he pulled up outside she reached quickly for the door handle.

'Well, I hope your takeover deal goes well for you.' She smiled at him. 'And I'll see you around some time.' She'd been practising the goodbye line for the last few miles and she was pleased that it sounded casual enough.

She hadn't intended waiting for his reply, but his voice held her back as she turned away.

'Haven't you forgotten something?'

'Have I?' She looked back at him with a frown.

'An invitation for coffee would be good.'

Her heart rate increased. She didn't really know how to handle this situation. Part of her was desperately pleased he wanted to come in with her and the other side of her was telling her fiercely to walk away now and not prolong the agony of wanting him...

'I don't think it's a good idea.' She lifted her chin a little.

'I think it's a very civilized idea.' He smiled. 'Let's not be awkward around each other, Carrie. I'm thirty-four and a man of the world. You're twenty-two and a virgin and I respect you for that.'

Her face flamed with colour.

'Besides, I'd like my shirt back.' His eyes flicked with wry amusement to the garment he'd given her to wear. It drowned her slender frame, yet she still managed to look sexy in it... How was that?

'I'll wash it and give it to Theo for you.' She tipped her chin up a little higher.

'No need, just give it back to me now.' Why did he love teasing her so much? he wondered as he watched the consternation and the fire in her beautiful eyes.

She turned away and got out of the car. 'I suppose you'd better come in, then.'

The grudging invitation made him smile and he reached for his phone and followed her.

The inside of the apartment was basic but pleasantly decorated. From his seat at the breakfast bar Andreas could see into a bedroom that contained two single beds.

He switched his attention back to Carrie as she flicked the kettle on. Her hair had dried in long flowing curls; she looked like a girl from a Pre-Raphaelite painting, young and yet somehow incredibly fragile as she looked over at him.

'I'll just change out of this shirt.'

He nodded and watched as she disappeared into the bedroom and closed the door. He would leave as soon as he'd had a coffee and she'd returned the shirt, he vowed. He had no business pursuing a virgin. Happily ever after wasn't for him, never would be. And something told him that innocent Carrie wouldn't really want to settle for less.

A few minutes later she reappeared wearing a blue fitted T-shirt over jeans and put his shirt down on the table beside him. 'Thank you.' Her voice was stiffly polite.

'My pleasure,' he replied and smiled to himself as she turned hurriedly to make the coffee.

She looked great in the jeans, they curved over her bottom, emphasizing how pert and toned she was.

He still wanted her. What the hell was the matter with him? he wondered angrily. He knew a million women with great figures—so what was he doing here? He should be heading back to his office. There was a mountain of paperwork waiting for his attention.

Yet still he sat on. *Because he was more intrigued by Carrie than ever.*

She put the coffee down in front of him just as his phone rang and he answered it impatiently.

'Now you know why I suggested going out to sea today,' he told her with a smile as he ended the call a few moments later.

'Theo told me that you never stopped thinking about business,' she said as she took the seat opposite him. 'I take it you enjoy it.'

He shrugged. 'It's become a way of life, I suppose. We grew up in Athens in complete poverty and I vowed back then that I wouldn't rest until I'd got us out of it.'

Carrie met his gaze. 'And obviously you did that.'

The simplicity of the statement made him laugh. 'Yes. But the thing is, the deeper you get involved with business, the more the responsibilities spiral.' He didn't tell her that he employed a lot of people, that he was backing Theo with an expansion plan for his diving business or that he'd just bought his father a house back on the island of Mykonos.

'It's addictive, you mean.'

'I don't think I'd go as far as to say that, but I like the challenge.'

She nodded. 'And I suppose being single and without children it's easier to immerse yourself in it, take bigger risks along the way.'

'I suppose it is…' He fell silent, her insightful remark taking him aback.

'My father was a wheeler-dealer in his day. But never gave a thought to his responsibility for others.' She frowned as she thought about her childhood. 'He was always looking for the next big deal.'

'And was he successful?'

'At first—but unfortunately he didn't know where to stop. Contentment wasn't a word he understood and risk-taking became a way of life.'

'He went bankrupt?'

She nodded. 'Yes. Took one risk too far and lost everything.' For a moment she fell silent. The personal cost had been even higher than the financial one. Her mother's health had crumbled and so had their marriage. Carrie had only been ten but she remembered the trauma and the feelings of helplessness as sharply as if it had been yesterday.

She pushed the silky weight of her long hair back from her face, trying to dismiss the memory. 'However, he was forever the optimist. He's probably out there somewhere right now looking for the next big deal.'

Andreas frowned. 'I assumed that your parents were both dead. Jo told me that you grew up together in a foster home.'

'We did. But my circumstances were different to Jo's. I wasn't orphaned. My mother died, but my father decided to go off looking for his fortune elsewhere and having a ten-year-old along with him was a bit of a handicap. So he left me to social services.'

She saw the look of shock on Andreas's face and shrugged.

'Some people aren't cut out to be parents, are they? And in the long run he probably did me a favour.'

Behind the brave words he heard the edge of sadness in her tone. 'Do you know where he is now?' he asked gently.

'I think he's in the States. I tried to trace him a few years ago and found out he was in Chicago and that he'd remarried. I left my contact details for him, but he never got in touch.'

'Some men don't deserve families,' Andreas muttered.

'Well, it worked out OK,' Carrie continued swiftly, 'because I met Jo and we are like family. She's the sister I never had, if you know what I mean.'

'Yes, I know what you mean.' He smiled.

His phone rang again and impatiently Andreas flicked it open and answered it.

Carrie finished her coffee and tried not to allow her eyes to linger on him. She couldn't believe that she had just opened up and told him all about her family! It was crazy. One moment he infuriated her…the next she felt as if she could melt in the warmth of his gaze…

He hung up and glanced across at her. 'Unfortunately I'm going to have to go.'

'Yes, of course.' She tried desperately to mask her disappointment. It was for the best—she didn't want to be a notch on anyone's bedpost, even someone as good-looking and enthralling as him. And at least by having this coffee together they'd broken the awkwardness between them, so that if they had to meet again due to Theo and Jo it would be tolerable. Maybe that was why he'd wanted to come in.

She stood up and walked with him towards the door. 'Thanks for an…interesting afternoon.' She'd been going to say enjoyable afternoon and thought better of it.

'Maybe we can do it again some time.'

'Who knows?' She tried to match his flippant tone. 'Maybe if you are passing and I'm in, we could fit another coffee between phone calls.'

'Perhaps, then, I should just say goodbye for now, Carrie. But I'm sure I'll be seeing you again soon.'

And then he was gone, striding away from her without a backward glance. So damn arrogant, she thought angrily, yet somehow utterly irresistible.

CHAPTER FOUR

CARRIE OPENED THE BLUE shutters and bright sunshine flooded into the cool interior of her apartment.

It was Sunday morning, the last day of her holiday and time to go home. Somewhere a church bell was tolling, the sound echoing down the narrow cobbled streets of the village. Carrie leaned against the window sill and allowed the heat and the tranquillity of the morning to wash over her.

She'd thought Andreas would have come to her last night, that he would have wanted to make the very most of their last evening together—but he hadn't. Of course he'd happily seen her over the past few days, on his terms! She hadn't been able to say no when he'd invited her out to dinner a couple of days after their trip to the reef. Nor had she had the strength to refuse his subsequent invitations. The truth was, she was wildly attracted to him, and she'd naively jumped at every chance to spend time getting to know him.

And now he'd seemingly tired of her. She didn't know whether to feel sad or just plain angry. He could at least have had the decency to phone her and tell her he wouldn't see her before she left.

But what did she expect, she asked herself furiously, when it was just a holiday fling and Andreas was a busy man?

Carrie raked a hand through the long length of her blonde hair as she thought back over the holiday. So much had happened—including the momentous news of Jo and Theo's engagement. And Jo had taken the decision to remain in Greece.

The four of them had enjoyed a celebratory dinner two nights ago. It had been a very joyful occasion. Carrie was going to miss her friend, but she was so happy for her.

But she hadn't seen Andreas since.

After the dinner he'd told her he was too involved with work to make a definite next date, and that he'd ring her.

That was the last she'd heard from him.

She wished now that she had never got involved with him—had never allowed herself to start believing that he might actually care about her. Especially when he'd made it quite clear up front that he wasn't looking for a serious relationship.

At least she hadn't been stupid enough to sleep with him.

But how much of that decision had been down to her good sense and how much had been down to his restraint, a traitorous little voice asked her mockingly. Because she did want him, in fact so much so that she ached for him. *And he knew that.* There had been a few times when he had kissed her at the end of an evening and she had been a whisper close to just begging him to sate her.

She turned away from the view of red-tiled rooftops and shimmering blue sea. It was just as well he hadn't come to her last night—because she might have done something she would have regretted.

She'd had a narrow escape, she told herself angrily as she glanced at her watch. Obviously the man couldn't really care less about her! If he did he would at least have phoned her last night to say goodbye.

It was time to start packing. Jo would be here to give her a lift down to the ferry terminal in an hour.

Carrie could hardly believe that Jo wasn't going to come back to London with her. It was going to be so strange not having her around any more, but she had no doubt that her friend was doing the right thing; Theo was such a nice, steady and reliable kind of guy.

The same could never be said of Andreas, she thought disparagingly. He spoke about commitment and love as if they were things to be avoided at all costs. And he'd obviously broken hearts by the truckload.

Yet he had been genuinely pleased for his brother and Jo.

She couldn't quite work him out.

Not that she wanted to work him out, she told herself firmly. Their relationship was never going to be anything as serious as Theo and Jo's. Neither of them were ready for settling down, it was the wrong time, the wrong place. Andreas was totally consumed with his business deal and she was too wary to commit herself to just a holiday romance—she had a good job to go back to.

So why did she feel like this? she wondered angrily as she got her suitcase out and started to pack. Why had she waited and waited last night for her mobile to ring?

Somehow over the last week reality had been swept away on a tide of emotion that she had never experienced before. Maybe it was something to do with the beauty of the surroundings and the way Andreas had wined and dined her; perhaps she had even been caught up with the mood of romance that surrounded Jo and Theo she thought rationally as she folded T-shirts and shorts.

And then she remembered the way Andreas could kiss her and her hands stilled. Deep down she knew her feelings weren't anything to do with their surroundings, Andreas's attentive generosity or even Theo and Jo's wonderful love for each other. It was the way Andreas made her feel. The way he'd been able to send shivers of pleasurable anticipation through her with just a look. The way he could kiss her and set her totally on fire.

No one had ever done that to her before.

But she wasn't stupid; she'd tasted the danger in his kisses, knew that beneath the charming urbane exterior there was the steely heart of the predatory male.

He was the type of man who would normally have made her

run for the hills, yet something strange had happened when he'd touched her; he terrified her, yet he'd captivated her.

And because he had treated her with restraint and respect she'd even started to imagine that she meant something to him… Stupid, she told herself as she started to fling clothes into her suitcase now without bothering to fold them. The sooner she got away from here and back to reality, the better.

There was a knock on the door and Carrie glanced at her watch. Jo was early! The realization that it was almost time to say goodbye to her best friend struck through her like ice.

'I wasn't expecting you for another hour…' Her voice drifted off as she swung the door open and found that it wasn't Jo, it was Andreas outside. Surprise and pleasure flooded through her. 'Oh…it's you!'

Hastily she tried to pull herself together. Every time she saw him she couldn't believe how gorgeous he was. But didn't he just know it, she reminded herself quickly as his dark intense eyes seem to sear into her and he smiled that confident smile of his.

He was wearing a suit and a blue shirt that was open at the neck, and he looked as if he'd come straight from a business meeting. It made Carrie feel very self-conscious about her own dishevelled appearance.

'I wasn't expecting you!' She tightened the belt of her blue silk robe. 'I thought it was Jo.'

'Are you disappointed?' he asked teasingly.

She didn't respond to the warmth of the enquiry. He was so damn sure of himself, she thought with a dart of anger. 'I'm just surprised,' she answered instead as she stepped back to allow him in. 'When I didn't hear from you yesterday I thought you'd probably forgotten that I leave today.'

'No, I didn't forget. I just got tied up with business in Athens.'

She noticed he didn't bother to try and apologise—didn't try to explain why he hadn't phoned her when he had said that he would.

As he moved further into the room his glance moved to the open door and the suitcase on the bed.

'You're lucky to have caught me,' she said lightly. 'I leave in an hour.'

He turned to face her and as their eyes connected she could feel the chemistry swirling between them like a living entity... entwining around her heart, enticing her with invisible strings to step closer into his arms.

It took all of her self-control to stay where she was.

She had her pride, and he was probably only here to say goodbye. 'So how is business going?' she asked lightly. She wasn't really interested; it was just something to say—something to cover the overwhelming feelings of need and confusion swirling inside her.

'Hard to tell. It's early days.'

She nodded. 'Theo told me last night that you were at a delicate stage of negotiation.'

'Did he?' Andreas shrugged nonchalantly.

His laid-back attitude stung. She'd suspected last night that Theo was making excuses for his brother's absence—but at least he had been trying to spare her feelings! 'I hope the deal works out for you,' she murmured, 'but you know what I think about high-risk ventures.'

He looked amused. 'Well, luckily I haven't come to discuss my business strategies with you, Carrie.'

'Haven't you?' She glared at him and raised her chin defiantly. 'So what are you here for?' she asked angrily.

To her surprise he reached out and took hold of her arm... pulling her closer. 'I've come for this...'

Before she could move away, his head was lowering, his lips capturing hers in a fiercely possessive kiss. She tried not to respond—she was upset at his high-handed manner...still reeling inside from the way he had just ignored her for the last two days.

But, hell, he could kiss and she wanted him so badly, and

before she realized what she was doing she was kissing him back hungrily.

Slowly she started to wind her arms up and around his neck.

'That's better.' He murmured the words with satisfaction as his hand stroked under the silk of her gown, finding the curve of her breast. 'This is *our* unfinished business…everything else doesn't matter.'

Her eyes closed on a wave of ecstasy as his fingers stroked provocatively over her. But even as she started to give herself up to the pleasure of his caress her mind was still whirring. Everything else did matter. As much as she wanted this, she couldn't shut out reality—he had ignored her for two days with not even the courtesy of a phone call, and her air ticket for home was sitting on the bedside table.

The reminder enabled her to pull away from him and draw the silk of her gown closer around her naked body. 'Andreas, I leave in less than an hour.'

'Yes—I realize that. But as I was saying, we've got unfinished business.' He looked at her with dark brooding eyes. These last couple of days he had purposefully distanced himself from her—told himself that it was for her sake as well as his own. She was so young, her whole life stretching ahead of her, and if she stayed and they got deeply involved, pretty soon she'd want a level of commitment from him that he was unwilling—unable—to give.

He was at a crossroads—a place he didn't want to be. He'd been heavily involved in a relationship once before and it had been a big—no, *huge*—mistake. He wasn't going down that route again.

'Andreas, I don't think you heard me. I leave for England in an hour.' She repeated her words fiercely, her eyes wide blue pools of shimmering emotion.

And suddenly he knew that, however selfish it was, he couldn't let her go. 'So why don't you tear up that air ticket and stay?'

Carrie stared at him. The quiet words made her heart pitch

with so much emotion that for a few seconds she couldn't think straight, and deep down she realized she'd wanted him to say those words to her…wanted it so desperately and so unrealistically that she hadn't even dared to voice the thought to herself.

But close on the heels of happiness there was wariness.

She remembered how he'd told her he could only offer her a casual affair—remembered how she'd waited over these last couple of days just for the telephone to ring.

If she said yes to Andreas would she be placing herself in a relationship where she came second to business? It certainly seemed so.

She tried to dismiss the fear, but the sensible side of her wouldn't let her.

OK, he'd asked her to stay, but she was all too aware of the things that had been left unsaid. What had changed between telling her that he didn't want a serious relationship and now?

'Why?' She raised clear unwavering eyes to his and he looked at her as if he couldn't believe the question. 'What are you thinking?' she continued quickly. 'In what capacity do you want me to stay?'

'I would have thought it was obvious. I want *you*…Carrie…' The words were said almost coolly…dispassionately. But there was nothing cool about the way his eyes raked over her. 'I want you in my bed. I want to teach you all there is about making love…morning, noon and night. Is that specific enough?'

The way he had just looked at her had fired her blood… *She wanted him too*. But his words weren't enough to banish the doubt churning inside her. And she realized suddenly that she had wanted him to tell her he had feelings for her and that he had started to fall in love with her. How naïve was that? she mocked herself fiercely. She really had lost all sense of reality!

Her eyes held with the darkness of his. He'd laugh if he knew what was going through her mind. She'd laugh herself only she was too deeply shocked by her own stupidity—and yet even now she felt a connection to him that was so deep that she couldn't quite unhook herself from it.

He didn't have time for deep emotion, she reminded herself firmly. He was too busy putting all his energies into business… playing for much higher stakes than love.

Could she really give up the good job that was waiting for her in London for this kind of uncertainty?

She took a deep breath, suddenly scared. 'I'm sorry, Andreas…but maybe on balance it would be best if I went back to London.' The words sounded stiff and staccato on her tongue. They weren't the words she wanted to say…but they were the ones she *had* to say. She couldn't give everything up for a man who put her second, a man moreover who liked to live dangerously where business deals were concerned—the lessons of growing up with someone like that were too deeply ingrained to ignore.

For a moment she saw surprise in his eyes. He'd expected her to just accept his terms, without any promises or even soft words. His arrogance was rather galling.

'Unlike you I'm not a person who likes to take risks,' she continued swiftly. 'I've been offered an extremely good job in London—one that I've worked hard to get. Even if I just stay there for a short time I need to take it.' She pulled the silk of her robe even closer around her slender body in an almost instinctively protective gesture as his eyes seemed to darken to deepest midnight. 'And maybe we need some space to think about things.' She added the words huskily, unable to bear the thought of completely closing the door on them. 'You're consumed with this business deal—who knows how we will feel about each other in another, say…six months' time?'

'You are quite a tease, aren't you, Carrie?' he cut across her suddenly, his eyes narrowing as rage started to simmer inside him. 'What you're really saying is that you want to keep your options open.'

'That's not what I'm saying at all!' Her skin flared with

colour. 'Come on, Andreas. You are in no position to throw that kind of accusation at me! You are totally focused on this deal of yours. You said yourself you don't want a relationship; you just want to take me to bed because…' Her voice trailed away in sudden embarrassment.

'Because you are a virgin.' He finished the sentence for her and watched as her skin caught fire. 'And you're right, I do prize the fact that you are a virgin.' He put a hand under her chin, tilting it so that he could look at her. 'And I've respected you for it.'

Their eyes held and silence seemed to simmer between them.

'But then you know that, don't you, Carrie? And you've used it to your advantage.'

'I don't know what you mean!'

'Well, let me spell it out. If you are waiting for me to propose marriage, it's not going to happen. I can't offer you that kind of commitment—it's not who I am.'

The cold, arrogant comment made her eyes widen with fury and gave her the strength to pull away from him. 'Well, it's a good job, because it's not who I am either. I'd have turned you down flat.' She gave a shaky incredulous laugh. 'I don't want a marriage proposal from you! I'm an intelligent woman, not a naïve fool. And we hardly know each other, for heaven's sake.'

'Good, we are both of the same mind, then. And I know very well that you are an intelligent woman, Carrie.' His voice was quiet, his gaze flicking over her, noting the rise and fall of her chest, the way she moistened her lips as his eyes touched them. 'I also know that you want me…'

The husky, confident words made her senses swirl. He was right she did.

There was still a part of her that wanted to say, Yes, OK, let's give this a whirl, *but for what*? She certainly didn't want a marriage proposal from him, but she did need more from him emotionally than he seemed prepared to give.

She hated his cold arrogance—hated the way he could look

at her like that, tell her he just wanted her for his bed, and still turn her on.

If she stayed, she could end up as a kept woman totally dependent on his every whim! She wouldn't even be able to get a decent job because she didn't speak Greek.

And then he could simply discard her for his next conquest when he got bored and she would be left without any fallback position.

She took a deep breath.

'The timing isn't right for us, Andreas, and we both know it.'

The fact that she could look at him with such emotion in her eyes, such warm need, and yet still turn him down enraged him; it also reminded him forcibly of things he didn't want to remember. Such as how he had no right asking her to fulfil his needs when he could never meet hers.

He'd made a mistake coming here. Asking her to stay had been crazy and he'd known that all along. Even if he just made her his mistress he would be in too deep—before he knew it they would be back at this crossroads and the relationship would have to end. Better that it was done now. He should have done it days ago, he told himself angrily, for her sake as well as his. He needed to burn all bridges and forget her.

'And when would you deem the time to be right, Carrie? When my business deal has paid off? Are you planning to save your virginity for the highest bidder?'

'I can't believe you've just said that!'

He was unrepentant as he watched the furious fires of anger and hurt burn in her beautiful eyes. *He needed to do this.*

'Don't worry about it, Carrie—we've had a bit of fun. And you were right, your innocence did intrigue me—I admit I wanted you and I know that, despite what you might say, you wanted me too.'

Carrie felt as if he had just struck her. 'Yes, well, hell would have to freeze over before I'd stay here and be stupid enough to give myself to someone like you!' she retaliated furiously.

He smiled. 'Actually, that's not true. I know I could have had you any time.'

With that he turned for the door, leaving her speechless with rage.

CHAPTER FIVE

Two years later

CARRIE stood out on deck as the high-speed ferry skipped across the glittering blue of the sea. In the distance she could see the small island of Pyrena drawing closer, shimmering in the hazy heat of the Greek sunshine, and memories tumbled painfully through her mind.

It was two years since she had first come here on holiday with Jo. And she could still recall every detail of that summer so vividly it was as if it were just yesterday.

Now it was hard to believe that Jo wasn't going to be waiting for her on that quay.

Even though they'd been mainly apart for the last couple of years the strong and enduring bond of friendship between them had never been broken. Jo had always been there in the background with emails and phone calls...

And Carrie had been back to visit her on the island three times and on each occasion Jo had been waiting eagerly for her.

And now she was dead...and Carrie could hardly bear it.

The island was clearer now; Carrie could see the familiar purple mountains, the secluded golden bays, the stunning scenery inevitably reminding her of Andreas, and the time they'd spent together.

Hastily Carrie turned her mind away from that. She didn't

like to think too deeply about Andreas. Even under happier circumstances the recollections of him made her emotions twist—which was crazy considering it had meant nothing, whereas Jo and Theo's relationship had been the real thing.

The last time Carrie had visited the island had been just after Jo had given birth to her daughter six months ago. The couple had been ecstatic and more in love with each other than ever.

Lilly's christening had been only three weeks ago, a time of celebration and happiness.

Carrie hadn't been able to make the christening. She'd been dealing with a vitally important contract at work and her boss had refused to give her the time off, had needed her to go to Hong Kong to sort things out for him.

But Jo had still wanted her to be Lilly's godmother, and had arranged it in her absence.

'I can't think of anyone I'd rather have to watch over my precious little girl,' she'd told Carrie in their last conversation. 'We may not be blood relatives but you are a part of my family and this is very important to me.'

It had been important to Carrie too—she'd taken the honour very seriously.

And now the words kept playing over and over in her mind. Because by the time she'd got back from Hong Kong to London there had been a letter waiting for her telling her that Jo and Theo had been involved in a car crash and that they'd both died instantly. The letter had been dated just four days after the christening.

The view of Pyrena blurred under the weight of Carrie's tears. Firmly she brushed them away. Since receiving the news from Jo's solicitor she had done nothing but cry and it wasn't helping. She had to be practical now, for Lilly's sake.

Jo and Theo had no family except for Andreas. Lilly was with him at the moment. But Carrie was worried about the situation, because, as she well knew, Andreas wasn't a family man; a six-month-old baby wouldn't fit into his bachelor life!

And, besides, by the sounds of things he was still as deeply involved with business as ever. Certainly every time she had visited the island he'd been away overseeing some important deal or other.

So what would become of Lilly, orphaned and alone?

The question had kept Carrie awake at night. And it haunted her days now. In desperation she'd even got Andreas's number from the solicitor and rung to see if he could shed any more light on the matter.

It had been her first contact with him in over two years. And the conversation had been very strained. Just thinking about it now made her temperature rise. He'd been very offhand with her.

For a few moments they had talked about Lilly and about Theo and Jo. And when Andreas had mentioned his brother's name there had been a raw note in his voice that had made tears immediately spring into her eyes. But he had cut short her whispered words of sympathy. And then he'd swept on and told her with brutal disregard for her feelings that there was no point in her coming back to Pyrena and that Lilly was none of her business!

The ferry slowed as it approached the harbour, and as the sea breeze died the heat of the day throbbed with an incredible force that almost matched the heat Andreas had stirred up inside her.

He always had been able to rouse extreme reactions within her. When they'd first met, those reactions had been purely passionate—an instinctive response to an extremely attractive man.

But back then she had been young and foolish. She'd learnt her lesson.

And if he thought she was going to stay away just because he told her to, he had another thought coming. Lilly was important to her and she was going to make damn sure she was all right!

What exactly that entailed Carrie wasn't sure. As she wasn't a blood relative she knew she had no rights, as Lilly's uncle, Andreas would ultimately be Lilly's guardian—all she knew was that Jo would have wanted her to do this and right now she was just allowing herself to be guided by instinct. She'd booked herself into a taverna near to where Andreas lived and from there she would evaluate the situation for herself, take it a step at a time.

The ferry was docking now, and there was a great deal of noise as the engines were reversed and men threw ropes to secure the vessel against the harbour wall.

Then the tailgate was lowered and the vehicles were driving off. Carrie lifted her case and followed the rest of the foot passengers down the gangplank.

She felt a tremendous sense of sadness as she walked out onto the harbour. It was like stepping back in time. She almost expected to see Jo standing at the side waiting for her, waving, smiling. Hastily she tried not to think about that, but instead concentrate on the fact that some things never changed: the fishing boats were still tied up alongside the wall, the old fishermen sitting next to them fixing their nets. Across the road there were a few whitewashed houses facing the jetty and then the parched fields criss-crossing into the distant misty mountainous interior. The heat was intense.

Carrie looked around for a taxi, but there wasn't one to be seen.

She was struggling with her high heels and her bag on the uneven terrain. She'd come straight from a business meeting in London this morning and, not only had there been no time to change, she hadn't even had time to organize her clothes properly the night before, due to a meeting in Edinburgh yesterday that had run late.

There was a bus at the end of the pier and she stopped next to it. 'Do you go to Phiorioous?' Carrie asked the driver, but he obviously didn't understand and just looked at her blankly. So did the old woman who was seated behind him with some chickens squawking in a basket.

Carrie put her bag down and looked around. It was amazing how quickly the crowds were clearing. One moment the harbour was teeming with activity—the next everyone was disappearing and the ferry was pulling out again.

And there was still no sign of any taxis. She tried again to communicate with the bus driver.

And that was where Andreas found her.

For a moment he just watched her from a distance, he couldn't believe how much she had changed.

The Carrie he had known two years ago had been dressed in tee shirts and shorts most of the time; she had been natural and tomboyish yet sexy and leggy with long blonde hair that had reached to her waist. This Carrie was so sophisticated that for a moment he hadn't even realized who she was. If not for the fact that she was so attractive that he'd given her a second look, he wouldn't have recognized her at all.

The blonde hair had been chopped into a modern shoulder-length style and she had pinned it back. A straight linen skirt and a crisp white blouse had replaced the shorts and T-shirt, and she was wearing killer high heels that emphasized her long legs and slender curves to full advantage.

'Do you go to Phiorioous?' she was saying slowly to the driver to no avail.

'I don't think he does,' Andreas drawled. 'And it's pronounced Persephone.'

She turned slowly.

Meeting his dark, intense eyes was such a complete shock that for a moment Carrie just stared at him wordlessly.

She didn't know what dazed her most: coming face to face with Andreas again so suddenly after two long years, or the fact that he could still churn her emotions into the consistency of melted butter.

For a moment neither of them spoke.

Carrie's first thoughts were that he hadn't changed at all, and that he looked fantastic.

He still made the blood pound through her veins with a force that made her feel dizzy, still stirred every sense within her creating chaos. And he was still the most handsome man she had ever met.

His lightweight suit sat perfectly on his broad-shouldered frame; his hair was jet dark, his eyes still as sexy and boldly enticing. However, it was only when she looked closer that she could see the faint lines etched round those dark eyes, and she knew him well enough to know that Theo's death had hit him hard.

'Hello, Andreas.' Her voice, when she finally found it, sounded stiff and awkward. 'What are you doing here?' She didn't know what else to say, she was so surprised to see him.

'I'm meeting you. What do you think I'm doing here?'

The sardonic, teasing tone was achingly familiar.

'Really?' After the way they had parted—and his reaction to her on the phone—she was stunned. Maybe like her he'd decided Lilly's welfare came first, she reasoned. Certainly she wouldn't have picked up the phone to him in a million years if it hadn't been for Lilly. She smiled hesitantly. 'That's good of you, I didn't expect you to pick me up.'

Andreas knew that smile so well and it seemed to twist into him like an instrument of sweet torture. How could she still affect him like that? he wondered irritably. 'Carrie, you made a point of telling me what time your flight was getting into Athens,' he reminded her brusquely. 'And there is only one ferry after that. So I decided—probably against my better judgment—that I'd oblige and put my chivalrous hat on.'

'I wasn't making any point!' She was horrified by the suggestion. Their telephone conversation had been so strained that she had told him about her travel arrangements merely to convince him that she was indeed coming! 'And I certainly didn't expect you to pick me up! Although why it should be against your better judgement I don't know!' She tilted her chin up a little, her blue eyes wide.

'Don't you?' He looked momentarily amused. 'I was referring to the fact that like petrol and a spark we tend to combust.'

The reply made her skin start to scald with heat. Was he referring to the way sparks had flown at their last meeting—or the sexual explosion of need that they had both tried so hard to control?

She really didn't want to think about that—it was far too unsettling! 'Don't worry, Andreas, any history we have is long forgotten,' she assured him huskily.

For a moment the darkness of his eyes held with hers and there was a look in their depths that was difficult to gauge.

Hastily she looked away. It was strange how he could still make her feel overwhelmed, naïve, and out of her depth. She wasn't the same person who had come here two years ago, she reminded herself fiercely. She was experienced in life now—a successful career woman, able to face the world on her own terms and survive. And Andreas had taught her a valuable lesson—that feeling passion for someone wasn't the same thing as feeling love.

The memory gave her the strength to face up to him. 'I'm only here for one reason—and that's Lilly.'

He inclined his head. 'And I'm here to pick you up for that self-same reason.'

'Well, at least we agree on something.'

'Yes.' He shrugged. 'But as I told you on the phone, I can't see what you hope to achieve by coming here for a quick visit.' His eyes seemed to pierce into hers. 'However…as I am short of childcare, I figured you may as well make yourself useful for a few days.'

'Oh! So that's why you're down here playing at being chivalrous!' Her eyes sparkled with annoyance. 'Well, let me assure you, Andreas, there is every point to my coming back—I'm Lilly's godmother and I will not be brushed aside as if I mean nothing. For one thing, Jo's solicitor asked me to come; I'm an executor of the will. And I intend to look out for Lilly's interests.'

'Good for you. Hopefully you can achieve all of that in your three-day visit…' Again there was that acrid tone in Andreas's voice.

'I'm here for a week, actually. I intend to stay on for a few days after the will is read.'

'Wow, a whole week!' His lips curved derisively. Then he looked at his watch. 'Carrie, I haven't got all day. Are you going to accept my offer and get into the car or not?'

Her glance moved past him to the very expensive open-topped sports car that waited. She wanted to tell him to go to hell, that she would rather fry in the sun for the rest of the day than take a lift with him—he was so damn infuriating.

But there was no point in antagonizing Andreas, not when they had Lilly's future to discuss. And, besides, the bus engine had flared into life behind her and the vehicle was pulling away. They were the only two people left on the pier now.

'Well, seeing as there are no taxis—I suppose *against my better judgement* I'd better accept your *kind* offer.'

For a second his lips curved in a smile. She hadn't changed at all, he observed. She always had been fiery, temperamental and hauntingly beautiful—and somehow she had managed to get under his skin in the past in a way that still bothered him now. The acknowledgement sizzled through him as he watched her pick up her suitcase.

What the hell was the matter with him? he wondered irately. All that was over with.

Yet he couldn't stop his eyes from flicking slowly over her, noting her sensual curves. Her proportions were still perfect, high, thrusting full breasts, a narrow hand-span waist, gently curving hips and legs that were long and shapely. He'd found her highly desirable two years ago, but to his consternation he found her even more alluring now. She seemed to have flowered into the epitome of womanhood.

At least she was a welcome distraction from the grief that had consumed him over the last few weeks, he thought grimly.

He watched for a moment as she struggled with her case, and then reached to take it from her to swing it easily into the trunk.

'Thanks.' She muttered the word through clenched teeth as she got into the car and slammed the door closed.

He took his jacket off and slung it onto the back seat of the car before getting in and turning the key in the ignition.

Silence fell between them as he drove out onto the road.

Carrie tried to concentrate on the countryside, tried to pretend that she wasn't completely on edge and aware of every detail of the man.

He was the only person she had ever met who seemed to ooze sex appeal and yet at the same time intimidate her completely. The type of man who always had to be in control, always had to be right—always got exactly what he wanted when he wanted.

But not with her, she reminded herself. And she was damn glad that she had resisted him after the way things had ended between them.

She just wished that she didn't still find him so attractive. She slanted a sideways glance at him and noticed how the loose-fitting white shirt he wore was ruffling in the breeze against the wide breadth of his hard, powerful chest. His lean body was perfectly honed. At thirty-six he was a man definitely in his prime.

Hating herself for even noticing, she took a deep breath and looked firmly away, she needed to concentrate on why she was here.

'So how is Lilly?'

'As I said on the phone, she's doing OK at the moment.' For the first time there was no biting edge to Andreas's tone. 'Last week she was very unsettled—not hungry—not sleeping.'

Just thinking about that small vulnerable child made Carrie's heart contract. 'She'll be missing her mum.'

Andreas glanced over as he heard the catch in her voice and hastily she looked away from him, fighting with herself not to lose control. It was amazing how grief worked, one moment she was all right and the next it just seemed to hit her out of nowhere. 'I haven't got my head around any of this,' she explained shakily. 'I was on a business trip when it happened and the first I knew of it was when I got home two days ago and found the solicitor's letter.'

He'd wondered why she hadn't been at the funeral. Andreas had made sure she'd been informed of the deaths, and he had scoured the churchyard for her. It had been almost inconceivable when she hadn't turned up.

'It's a difficult situation to accept,' he said quietly. 'They were both so young, had everything to live for.'

'And Lilly was everything to them.'

'Yes…' Andreas thought about the tiny child in his care and for a moment silence fell between them.

Life was bizarre. He'd never envisaged looking after a baby full time on his own—in fact his whole existence was mapped out in such a way as to not include a family. He'd long since abandoned any ideas of marriage and the trappings of domestic bliss; one bad relationship was enough to tell him he wasn't cut out for family life.

Although he was Lilly's uncle and godfather he'd only held her for the first time at the christening, and, while he'd loved her and thought she was delightful, he had been only too glad to hand her back to her parents. Therefore it had been a total shock to feel the fierce surge of protectiveness that had rushed through him when a nurse had placed the infant into his arms after the accident. Lilly had looked up at him with such wide trusting eyes, and the need to make things right for her, to take care of her, had overwhelmed him. It still did.

'I'm just thankful that she wasn't in the car with them,' Carrie murmured.

'Actually she was. She was strapped into her carrycot on the back seat.'

Carrie looked at him in horror. 'But she's OK?'

'Yes, she was thoroughly checked over and there wasn't a scratch on her. Obviously she's too young to realize what has happened, but I think you're right. I think what's wrong with her at the moment is that she is missing her mother. Jo was with her all the time.'

Carrie nodded. 'Who's looking after her this afternoon?'

'My housekeeper.' Andreas glanced at the clock on the dashboard. 'Marcia is great—but she only works part time as she looks after her elderly mother. She's doing me a favour staying late today.'

It sounded as though things hadn't been easy and the situation was far from ideal. 'Well, now that I'm here I'll help in any way I can.'

'Will you indeed?' He glanced over with a raised eyebrow and for a second their eyes held.

And for some reason she felt herself go hot inside.

'Well…yes…I have Lilly's best interests at heart I assure you.'

He smiled. 'That's very good to know.'

There was a note in his voice that unnerved her slightly.

Andreas returned his attention to the road.

He'd known she would feel like that—his brother had told him how she'd doted over Lilly when she visited. And he'd found himself remembering those words after their uncomfortable telephone exchange the other day.

It was that memory that had made him revise his initial instincts that she should stay away. He'd realized he needed to put any personal feelings to one side and just take full advantage of this situation.

He needed someone to take care of Lilly whilst he advertised for staff and sorted things out. Needed someone he could feel confident about leaving her with whilst he caught up with work at his office. Carrie would do very nicely… He slanted a glance over at her; in fact she would do very nicely indeed…

They stopped at traffic lights.

He could smell the familiar scent of her perfume, a mixture of honeysuckle and clean linen. Strange how he could remember the fragrance so well—and with it the memory of her body, firm…hot…and, oh, so achingly innocent.

He wondered if she was still a virgin and then mocked himself. She was twenty-four, of course not!

For a moment he remembered the first time they had kissed. Her innocence and her passion had been a heady combination.

God, he had wanted her. His hands tightened on the steering wheel now as he thought about the feelings she had stirred inside him. How difficult it had been to pull back from her.

Then he remembered that last morning when he'd lost his senses completely and asked her to stay.

He could still recall the anger that had burnt through him when she had turned him down. And from time to time over the last couple of years when Jo had mentioned her name he had felt that same sharp stab of fury lingering. Why he should feel like that he didn't know. He respected her decision—hell, he'd gone with it, had finished things completely when he could have left them open.

Maybe the anger was down to the fact that she had brought out the hunting predatory instinct in him, posed a challenge. Dented his macho pride by turning him down.

His mistake, he shouldn't have cared about her being a virgin—should have just pressed his advantage when the time had been right. Because she *had* wanted him. He'd broken through her reserve on more than one occasion...brought her to the point of no return and then pulled back.

'It's hot, isn't it?' Carrie murmured, wishing the traffic lights would change, wishing the silence between them didn't feel so loaded.

He reached and turned the air conditioning up and then glanced over at her, noticing the way her hair was escaping in little tendrils around her face, how the top buttons of her blouse were strategically unfastened to give just a provocative glimpse of a whiter than white bra.

Sexually he still wanted her; the thought tore through him with brutal intensity.

He hadn't wanted to still feel like this about her—in fact it was the main reason behind his abrupt attempt at telling her not to come here.

But maybe it was time he finished what he should have finished two years ago.

Aware of his gaze resting on her, of the sudden feelings swirling between them, Carrie tried not to look over at him, not to meet his gaze, but something drew her, something she was powerless to resist. The chemistry between them seemed to implode into a million splintering pieces swirling between them with more intensity than the rays of the sun.

Frowning, she tried to tell herself that it was in her imagination. All of that was over with now. But as his eyes rested on the softness of her lips she remembered the first time he had taken her into his arms and kissed her. The unexpected and intense memory took her breath away as if someone had just pushed her over the edge of a cliff into a deep abyss. And as his eyes moved over her she wanted to feel his lips again…wanted it with an ache of need that almost made her gasp.

'Better?'

She stared at him, not understanding the question.

'Cooler with the air-conditioner turned up?'

'Oh…yes…thanks.' She was mortified by her thoughts and then even more dismayed when she noticed the arrogant gleam in the depths of his gaze and realized he knew exactly what effect he was having on her. Shaken, she looked away, her heart thundering as if she had been pursued for miles by a dangerous predator and then cornered. What was wrong with her? She needed to forget all about the past, she needed to concentrate solely on Lilly and on reality.

The traffic lights turned to green and Andreas put the car into gear and moved forward. There was a determined expression on his features now, the glimmer of a smile on the sensual curve of his lips.

Carrie tried very hard to regain her composure, pretend that the awkward moment hadn't happened. But somehow she couldn't.

The coastline appeared, and in front of them was the small town of Persephone; its quaint buildings perched on the very edge of the steep cliffs, dazzling white against the sparkle of the sea and the fierce, uninflected blue of the sky. She relaxed a little. They were very nearly at her destination.

'You can just drop me off anywhere down by the quay here,' she told him, anxious to be away from him as quickly as possible. 'I've booked into the taverna.'

The turn off for the village appeared, but Andreas drove straight past it.

'You've missed the road,' she told him with a frown.

'Yes, I know. I meant to miss it.' He kept on driving. 'Carrie, there is no point to you staying in the village.'

Surprise and consternation seemed to zing through her bloodstream. 'What on earth do you mean? I've chosen there especially so I can be close by for Lilly!'

'Well, you can be closer still,' he told her firmly. 'You can stay at my place.'

'I'm not doing that!' she answered instinctively, her voice taut with emotion, the thought of being in close proximity to Andreas for any length of time making alarm bells ring very loudly in her head.

He glanced over, noticing the wary look in her eyes now, and impatience flicked through him.

'I thought you said you wanted to help in any way you can?' he asked mockingly.

'I do…but…staying at your place isn't a good idea.'

'Why not?' His eyes seemed to taunt her. 'I need someone to watch over Lilly so I can catch up on some work. You want to spend time with her. I think this will suit both our purposes.'

Something about the way he said that made her nerves stretch tighter.

Andreas noted the heat rising under the creaminess of her skin and smiled. The more rattled she sounded and looked, the more it reminded him of the past. How she could look at him with heated passion one moment, then wide-eyed, defenceless kitten appeal the next.

In the past, that look had worked on him—*but not this time.* This time the playing field was levelled.

'To be clear, all I'm offering you is one of my spare bedrooms Carrie, not my bed.'

He watched how the blunt statement made her squirm.

'I didn't think anything else for a moment!' she told him quickly.

'Didn't you?' A smile curved his lips as he noticed her skin was on fire now. 'So no need to sound and look so edgy, then—unless of course you *want* to share my bed for a few days' recreational sex?'

'You always did have a reprehensible sense of humour, Andreas!' she flared.

He laughed. 'And you always were a sexy piece of work, Carrie.' He slanted her a fleeting look. 'You have matured rather nicely, I have to say,' he added.

She swallowed. 'Let's get back to the realms of reality, shall we? The important issue is Lilly.'

'Which is where I was before you looked at me with such…wide-eyed innocent hesitation.' He smiled, but his attention was firmly on the road now as it climbed and twisted, showing dizzying views across the sea. 'You moving in with me is just an extremely practical solution, I assure you.' And he meant that—the child in his care had to come first. Righting a mistake from the past would just be an added bonus.

Carrie hesitated. She knew the idea made sense, but the way he was wording it was giving her palpitations…especially after the unwanted memories and feelings that had just taunted her.

'Just a temporary arrangement,' he continued. 'Not perfect, but a short-term solution to meet all our needs.'

Carrie's heart was thudding uncomfortably in her chest as she fought with her innermost feelings. She did want to spend as much time as possible with Lilly. But…she didn't want to be alone with Andreas—no, more than that, she was *scared* of being alone with him.

Desperately she tried to quash the fear; it was foolish, illogical. Any feelings between her and Andreas were dead—any lingering chemistry she still felt was imagined. And for Lilly's sake she couldn't afford to consider the situation in any way other than realistically. This wasn't about *them*; this was about a parentless child.

But even so she couldn't help wondering about the atmosphere that had sprung up between them a few moments ago…a reaction that she had thought was long forgotten…that she didn't even want to acknowledge or put a name to.

Because if she did it would turn every minute under the same roof as Andreas into a very dangerous proposition indeed. 'Well, I suppose you are right—it could be a practical solution for a few days,' she murmured cautiously.

'Exactly.' Andreas smiled to himself as he swung the car through the gateposts to his home. *Checkmate*, he thought with satisfaction.

CHAPTER SIX

THE car rounded a corner and the driveway opened out to reveal a shimmering white mansion set in its own grounds. Carrie's eyes widened.

Jo had told her a few months ago in an email that Andreas had bought himself a fabulous new house, but she hadn't been expecting anything as opulent as this! This was the kind of place that graced the TV programmes about homes of the rich and famous, an ultra modern sprawling villa on two levels. It had an infinity pool that merged with the blue of the Mediterranean on one side and a helipad complete with helicopter on the other.

She supposed she shouldn't really have been surprised. She had always known that Andreas was phenomenally ambitious—totally focused on his goals. And she knew he had been successful, recently she had even read an article about him in the *Financial Times* that had lauded him as an astute businessman as sure footed as a cat and with about the same killer instinct.

He pulled the car to a halt by the front door and the silence and the heat of the late afternoon descended. Despite the fact that it was now nearing five-thirty the air was still sizzling, laced with the scent of the sea and the exotic flowers that scrambled across a trellis by the open front door.

'Beautiful place,' she reflected lightly as they both stepped out of the car onto the gravel drive. 'Seems you've achieved everything you wanted.' She couldn't resist the throwaway comment.

His gaze connected with hers. 'On the contrary, Carrie, I still have challenges ahead.' It was hard to tell exactly what was going through his mind; his features were emotionless, his eyes darkly intense, yet something about the way he said that made her senses prickle.

Then his lips curved in a sardonic smile. 'Let's go and see how Lilly is getting on, shall we?'

The sound of a child crying greeted them as soon as they stepped into the hallway and they followed the sound across the cool marble floor into one of the reception rooms.

Carrie only vaguely registered the beauty of the house, the cream brocade curtains that framed the views of the sea, the plush sofas and the stone fireplace that filled an entire wall; her whole attention was focused on the crib from where the crying was emanating and from where, with every second that passed, the cries turned into fiercer, more hacking sobs.

A middle-aged woman dressed in black was standing next to the crib rocking it, trying to calm the child and settle her with soothing words.

She turned as she heard the door open, and there was a look of relief on her lined face.

'Having problems, Marcia?' Andreas spoke to her in Greek.

'She's been crying for an hour—I have lifted her and walked with her and tried to feed her a bottle and still she cries.'

Carrie went across to look inside the cot.

Lilly's eyes were scrunched up with tears, her cheeks red, and her plump little legs kicking out angrily in the pink romper suit.

'Hello, darling, that's a lot of noise coming from someone so small.' Carrie leaned closer and stroked a hand over the side of her face wiping the tears away, and suddenly the crying stopped as if by magic and Lilly regarded her with wide blue eyes.

'That's better.' Carrie smiled at her through a sudden blur of her own tears. 'You've grown since last time I saw you, sweetie…and you know what? You look more like your mummy than ever.'

The child gurgled happily, little arms reaching upwards as she pleaded with Carrie to lift her up.

'You've made a hit,' Andreas remarked in surprise as he walked closer and watched the child's reaction to her. 'Marcia has just been telling me that she has tried everything and couldn't stop her crying.'

'Poor little thing.' Marcia spoke in English. 'She has been… what is the word? Inconsolable. And now look.'

They all watched as Lilly smiled and kicked and held her arms up towards Carrie, impatient to be lifted.

'Amazing! Well, she's too young to be able to remember you from your last visit, I'm sure.' Andreas leaned in and tickled the child affectionately and she giggled, obviously happy to see him. 'You are a little devil, aren't you, Lilly?'

'Maybe she likes your English accent,' Marcia suggested suddenly to Carrie. 'Perhaps you remind her of her mother.'

'Perhaps.' Carrie dragged her attention away from the child for a moment and smiled politely at the other woman.

'Marcia, this is Carrie Stevenson.' Andreas made the introductions swiftly. 'Carrie was Jo's closest friend.'

'I know. Jo has spoken of you many times.' The woman nodded. 'I'm so sorry for your loss.'

'Thank you.' Carrie blinked back more tears.

'Carrie is going to help look after Lilly for a few days whilst I sort out a more permanent solution to childcare,' Andreas told her.

Carrie looked into the cot and smiled at the little girl, who seemed to be listening now to every word Andreas was saying, her eyes wide and trusting.

A permanent solution to childcare… The words echoed inside her. They sounded clinical and cold. But she knew Andreas had to be practical.

'Thanks for looking after her this afternoon, Marcia. Hopefully we can start getting things back to normal around here soon,' he continued.

'Not a problem.' Marcia smiled.

What was normal around here? Carrie wondered. Probably Andreas away on business and out with different women all the time. Hastily she swallowed down the images of a life where Lilly was brought up by staff. She couldn't start leaping to those kinds of conclusions; she had only just arrived and she didn't really know what Andreas's plans were. Perhaps he intended to cut down his workload? As soon as that suggestion crossed her mind she rejected it as unlikely. Andreas was totally work orientated. Working less would be a complete anathema to him.

'Nice to meet you, Carrie.' Marcia nodded to her as she went to pick up her bag and take her leave.

'You too.' Carrie smiled back.

As Andreas walked to the front door with the other woman Carrie returned her attention to Lilly.

She was so small and helpless and so very like her mother, with the same deep blue eyes and blonde curly hair.

Lilly smiled and kicked her legs impatiently, holding her arms out to Carrie again.

'You really want out of there, don't you, sweetheart?'

Carrie reached in and lifted her up, holding the warm little body close.

She'd done the right thing coming here, the knowledge swirled inside her forcefully, along with the realization of just how much Lilly meant to her.

The child nuzzled closer and Carrie noticed the full bottle of milk sitting on the table.

'Are you hungry? Is that the problem?' She reached for the bottle and tested the temperature of the milk on the back of her hand, but it had gone cold. 'Come on, let's find the kitchen and sort you out.'

The hallway was deserted now; through an open doorway Carrie could hear Andreas talking on the phone. Probably taking the opportunity to get back to business as soon as he could, which reinforced her suspicions—there was no way he could cut back on work. She walked down the long hallway opening doors to peep inside.

The house had every modern amenity, even a gym! She wondered if that was how Andreas maintained his perfect body and then cut the thought short—she really didn't want to think about how good Andreas's body was.

She found the kitchen at the back of the house; it overlooked an immaculately manicured garden complete with another swimming pool and behind that a field of sunflowers. The sun was starting to go down, sending a blaze of pink light over the shimmering gold blooms.

Carrie didn't know which she was more impressed with: the view, or the extravagance of the kitchen. It was an enormous space and no expense had been spared: the counter tops were solid granite on buttery cream modern units; there was an enormous black and silver range cooker. Everything seemed pristine, as if it had never been used. She couldn't help but compare it with the kitchen in her flat, which was looking rather tired these days. She'd been away on business so much that it was hard to concentrate on décor; in fact she'd been working such long hours that it was hard to have the time to think about anything—even her social life, which had ground to a halt since her relationship with Mike had ended.

For a moment she thought about Mike, thought about how she'd perceived him as someone steady and reliable. She'd been extolling his virtues to Jo not long ago and the very next week after that conversation she'd found out he'd been two-timing her with his secretary!

She had been such an idiot to believe all the stuff he'd spouted about having real feelings for her. She was obviously an expert at misjudging men!

Lilly grizzled in her arms and she returned her attention to the important job of preparing more milk. She didn't want to think about Mike, she had more important things on her mind now! Carrie settled herself on one of the bar stools to feed Lilly and the child took the bottle eagerly; for a moment the silence was filled with her hungry little gulps. There was something strangely cathartic about the sound. London and her hectic job and Mike seemed a long way away.

Carrie kissed the top of Lilly's head, she smelt of baby shampoo and rosewater. 'Everything is going to be fine now, sweetheart,' she murmured softly.

But would it really? The question taunted her. What would a bachelor businessman know about looking after a six-month-old baby? Then again, what did she know about looking after babies? she asked herself sensibly. Really very little. She had no brothers or sisters—no first-hand knowledge of bringing up children at all. And Andreas was extremely wealthy, so therefore he would probably easily solve the problem.

But when she looked down at the child in her arms a different set of emotions swirled inside her—money didn't buy love.

So where did that leave Lilly?

The question made her stomach twist. She knew what it was like to be young and vulnerable and alone. When her mother had died there had been nobody to look after her. It had been a very traumatic time.

The couple that had eventually fostered her had been kind—but they'd had no real interest in her. They hadn't had time to listen to how she felt—how she missed her mother, and how she felt incredibly let down by her father. If not for the fact that Jo had been there, she didn't know how she would have survived.

For a moment she thought her heart would drown in tears as she remembered her tough, warm-hearted friend who had been through so much herself. And had been there for her when she needed her most.

She looked down at the child in her arms. 'What are we going to do with you?' she asked playfully, trying to lighten her mood and her tone.

Andreas heard Carrie's voice as he stepped out of his office, and instead of heading back towards the drawing room he followed the sound towards the kitchen. He stopped just inside the doorway and watched as Carrie fed Lilly her bottle; she was talking to the child in animated tones, telling her about her mother, telling her how much she was loved.

For a moment he stood and watched her through the open doorway. For a high-flying businesswoman she looked surprisingly at home, both in his kitchen and with Lilly cradled on her knee.

He noticed how her blonde hair had escaped its ties completely now, how it swung silkily as she reached for the clean bib that was sitting on the counter top. With her hair loose she looked incredibly young—just like the Carrie he had met for the first time two years ago, and yet there was a maternal womanliness about her that held him spellbound. Something about the way she looked at the child in her arms, the way she spoke with such tenderness, hit him with a mixture of emotions he couldn't begin to unravel.

All he knew was that he was glad he'd put aside his earlier reservations, because bringing her here today had been absolutely the right thing to do.

She was just what Lilly needed right now, and he felt a deep sense of satisfaction that he had judged that situation so correctly.

As he moved she looked around and their eyes met.

She was just what he needed right now too, he realized with a fierce thrust of desire. He wanted to blot out the last few weeks and pretend they had never happened, he also wanted to put the illusions of their past relationship firmly where they belonged—in the past. OK, Carrie had got under his skin last time, but that was only because he hadn't bedded her. Once they'd had some great meaningless sex all those illusions would be forgotten.

'How long have you been standing there?' she asked softly. There was a shimmer in her eyes—a look—a glance that intensified the feeling inside him.

Oh, yes, bringing Carrie here was definitely the right thing.

'Long enough to hear that you have been having quite a conversation.' Andreas moved further into the room.

'Just a little catch-up.' Carrie tried not to feel embarrassed and instead focused her attention on the child in her arms. But she was acutely aware of Andreas as he came closer and leaned against the counter next to her.

She could smell the scent of his cologne, could sense the rippling power of his muscles as he leant across and stroked a gentle hand over the side of the little girl's face.

'Whatever you are doing it seems to be working—she seems happier,' he said as he transferred his attention from the child to her.

'I hope so.'

He was too close, and in the fast-fading light of the kitchen she felt an intimacy about the situation that made her even more physically aware of him.

Deliberately she turned her thoughts once more to Lilly. 'But I think she's getting tired,' she murmured. 'What time do you usually put her down?'

'About seven.'

He looked at the child again. And they both watched as she struggled to keep her eyes open. Her interest in the remaining milk was decreasing, the hungry little tugs against the bottle growing fewer and fewer.

Carrie pulled the bottle away and Lilly didn't murmur; she was fast asleep. The rosebud lips were in a perfect little pout; dark lashes silky against the creamy skin.

'She's adorable, isn't she?' Carrie whispered, for a moment forgetting everything except the baby in her arms.

'Yes, she is.'

There was silence between them as they both watched the sleeping child. 'I just wish Jo and Theo were here...' The words fell huskily from her lips.

'So do I...believe me. But we can't change the past. Can't do anything now except our best for Lilly.'

It was strange how comforting she found the deep tone of his voice. Carrie almost longed to lean closer against him, have him embrace her. Her eyes lifted to his and then she jolted back to her senses. Looking for comfort from Andreas was about as crazy as wanting to have a cuddle with a crocodile.

Andreas reached to take the bottle from her and put it down on the counter, and then he unfastened Lilly's bib. 'Come on, let's take her upstairs. I'll show you where everything is.'

She nodded and allowed him to take the sleeping child from her, trying to ignore the shiver of awareness as his hand brushed against the bare skin of her arm.

Silently she followed him up through the darkness of the house. He didn't put any lights on until they reached the upstairs corridor, and then with one flick of a switch a few lamps threw a subdued glow that did nothing to lessen the tension swirling inside Carrie.

'I've put Lilly's cot in the dressing room that leads off my bedroom,' he told her as he strode ahead. 'That way I can listen out for her at night.'

Carrie held back as he turned through the doorway and her eyes swept cautiously over the sumptuous surroundings dominated by the most enormous double bed.

'Through here, Carrie,' he directed.

She tried not to look at anything as she followed him, tried to pretend she was anywhere else except in Andreas's bedroom. And she was so busy trying not to look at his bed that she almost fell headlong over her suitcase, sitting next to the bedside table.

'Andreas, what is my suitcase doing in your room?' She hoped her voice didn't sound as disconcerted as she felt, but even to her own ears the question seemed to come out in a high-pitched tone.

'You're sleeping in here tonight,' he told her dismissively. 'I've got to attend an early morning meeting in Athens so I could do with you being close at hand.'

'I see.' She tried to sound unconcerned. But the arrangement was sending goose bumps down her spine. She hovered in the doorway that led through to his dressing room, watching him as he placed the child gently down into her cot.

She noticed that an effort had been made to turn the space into more of a nursery by placing all of Lilly's toys on the shelves; she also noticed Andreas's clothes were hanging at the very end of the room.

'So…where are you going to sleep?' She forced herself to ask the question, and he looked up at her with amusement.

'Why? Are you going to come looking for me in the night?'

He saw the way she blushed and laughed. 'Don't worry, if you need me I won't be too far away—just across the corridor, in fact.'

He was so damn arrogant that it was maddening! 'I hate to burst your bubble but that's not going to happen,' she told him staunchly.

'What's not going to happen?' He tucked Lilly in and then turned to look at her and something about the teasing gleam in his eyes made her temperature start to soar.

He was deliberately provoking her, she realized suddenly, and enjoying it! She needed to be aware of that fact, and not give him the satisfaction.

'Let's not play games, Andreas,' she told him crisply.

'No, let's not.' He nodded. 'Because the time for games between us is long over.' There was a serious edge to the words that made her feel slightly breathless. And as he started to walk closer towards her she found herself backing away.

Something about the purposeful look on his face made her heart smash against her ribs, made her thoughts start to dissolve into complete panic.

She came to an abrupt halt as she found that she had backed away so much that she was in his bedroom, and his bed was directly behind her.

'We have Lilly to think about now and we need to focus completely on her, don't we?' she reminded him, tipping her chin up resolutely, forcing herself to concentrate on what was important and not on the effect he was having on her.

He smiled. 'It would certainly help if we could work together for this week.' He reached past her and as he did so his arm brushed against her breast, and instantly she could feel her body responding very positively to him. It was mortifying.

'You'll need this.'

She didn't know what she was expecting but it wasn't the neat pile of ironing that he placed into her arms. 'Clean linen… for my bed. Marcia didn't get a chance to change it this morning. She was too busy with Lilly.'

'Oh! OK!' She swallowed hard. She needed to get a grip, and turn her highly imaginative thoughts off, she told herself angrily. Andreas was just being practical. She put the sheets down on the bedside table next to her. 'Actually I think I'll turn in and have an early night.'

'At seven in the evening!' He sounded amused. 'You're not hiding from me, are you, Carrie?'

'Don't be silly. Why would I want to hide from you? I'm just tired that's all.' She looked away from him in case he saw the truth in her eyes, because he was right. She couldn't handle being in such close proximity to him. 'I had an early start this morning.'

He nodded. 'And unfortunately you will have another early start with Lilly tomorrow. But with a bit of luck she will sleep through the night. She did last night.'

Carrie was distracted suddenly as she noticed some framed photographs on top of a dresser. Some were of Lilly when she was just a few hours old—one was of Jo and Theo on their wedding day.

Andreas followed her gaze. 'Jo gave those to me,' he told her softly.

'She sent me some similar ones.' Carrie moved across to pick up the wedding photo. 'They look so happy.'

'Yes, it was a good idea their going away and getting married quietly on a beach. They loved St Lucia.'

'Jo was so excited,' Carrie reflected as she looked down at her friend's smiling face. She remembered the phone calls that had preceded their decision to cancel their church wedding. Jo had found out she was pregnant and was ecstatic, and neither she nor Theo had wanted to wait around for the big service they had originally planned. 'I'm so glad that they had that time together now and that they didn't wait.'

'Sometimes you just have to grab life, don't you? And they certainly did that with the short time they had with each other.' Andreas walked across and took the photo from her. Instinctively he reached and smoothed a stray strand of her hair back from her face. And for a moment it was as if time had turned back.

Carrie felt it too…a shift of mood so slight, so subtle, that it was hardly discernible until he touched her and then it was too late. And then she realized just how close she was to him, close enough to go back into his arms and lift her face for his kiss.

And she wanted to do that so much that it hurt.

'You haven't changed, Carrie,' he murmured huskily. 'Not at all… And there is still chemistry between us.'

'Don't, Andreas…' Her plea was almost inaudible. She didn't want him to say these things…and she was scared by how much he was turning her on, how much she wanted him; scared and yet unable to move away. 'We're not thinking straight… This isn't a good idea…'

He paid her whispered words no heed. Instead he lowered his head and his lips captured hers.

There was nothing sweet about the kiss. It was an almost fierce possession…and yet Carrie welcomed it…wanted it with a hungry, driving force that after the first few seconds of trepidation just seemed to overwhelm her.

It was as if some kind of madness possessed her totally; she found herself wanting to be even closer, found her hands reaching to stroke upwards over his chest to rest on his shoulders.

Andreas felt a deep searing triumphant satisfaction, mixed with a strange swirl of emotion. He could taste the salt of her tears and that, combined with the fragility of her initial response, floored him, opened a well of feelings that angered him. He didn't want to consider these emotions, or her vulnerability; he just wanted to drive out this insatiable, damnable thirst that he felt for her. Forget the past, forget everything…especially the one reason why it had been right to let her walk away from him.

He pulled back from her, leaving her breathless and dizzy, and she stared up at him with an almost dazed incomprehension.

'That shouldn't have happened.' Her voice was so shaky that it didn't even sound as if it belonged to her.

That she could dismiss her fiery response to him so swiftly and easily made a thrust of anger sear through him. 'On the contrary, maybe it was long overdue,' he grated. 'Don't beat yourself up about it, Carrie. It's called animal magnetism for a reason—it means that there doesn't have to be any emotion behind the feelings.'

The arrogant mocking words made her push away from him, and a feeling of shame scalded through her as she remembered how passionately she had returned his kisses. 'This had nothing to do with magnetism or anything else—you just caught me at a low ebb, that's all.' From somewhere she found the strength to rally.

'Is that what it was?' His voice twisted with derision. 'Well, I'm glad we cleared up the misunderstanding.' His gaze drifted over her slowly, taking in her flushed countenance, the softness of her lips.

The sensual look inflamed Carrie's reasoning and for one crazy moment she wanted him to reach for her again, kiss her again.

Andreas saw it in her eyes and he felt the tension starting to leave his body.

'You are as beautiful as ever, Carrie—and I think we still want each other as much as ever. We used to put it down to a moment of madness, didn't we?' he reflected gently. 'Back in the old days.'

'I don't want to talk about the old days, Andreas!' she told him quickly, her voice trembling as she remembered how things had finished between them back then. How she had longed for him to say some soft romantic words and talk about his feeling for her. But instead all he had talked about was taking her to bed!

How could she have allowed herself to kiss him after he had treated her like that? How could she allow herself to forget for one moment the hurt he had inflicted on that last day when he had mockingly admitted he had just wanted her for sex? Had she no pride? No self-respect?

'And, just so we are clear, I don't want you. In fact I feel nothing for you, Andreas!' She flung the words at him bitterly. '*Nothing*. I have a life back in London…a man who cares about me.' The white lie about Mike tripped off her tongue—better that Andreas knew that he had no chance of them picking up from where they'd left off before he'd so cruelly shattered her illusions two years ago.

Andreas looked unconcerned.

'And yet you can passionately kiss someone you say you feel nothing for? Maybe you need to think about that relationship back in London—maybe it's going nowhere.'

'I don't need to think about it!' she flared furiously. 'How dare you pass judgement on something you know nothing about?'

'Hey, it's none of my business! I was just trying to save you from making a mistake, that's all,' he replied laconically.

'Well, I don't need your help, thank you.'

'Fine.' He held her gaze for a few moments. And she remembered how much she had wanted him in the past. How she had found herself thinking about him, weeks, months, even years after the end of their brief encounter.

And he was right—Mike had never made her feel such intensity of emotion… No one had ever aroused passion in her like Andreas. She was still a virgin, for heaven's sake! Mike was the longest relationship she'd ever had—three months and she still hadn't been ready to sleep with him. It had always been surprisingly easy to pull away—to make excuses. Yet she'd wanted to be swept away by him, she'd believed he was a nice guy—she'd wanted to feel the passion that Andreas had stirred within her—but it just hadn't happened.

Andreas would probably laugh if he knew that—

She tried to push the disturbing thoughts away. 'I kissed you because I was upset and you were there…nothing more to it,' she told him fiercely now. 'So let's forget about it—OK.'

'You've heard that old adage, haven't you, about protesting too much?' Andreas smiled, and then before she could reply he walked away. 'Goodnight, Carrie, I hope you sleep well.'

As soon as the door closed Carrie sat down on the bed and buried her head in her hands. She hated herself for responding to him. But the really terrifying thing was how much she still wanted him!

If he could turn her on like that with just one kiss, what would it feel like to go to bed with him?

The question was profoundly tormenting…but it wouldn't go away.

CHAPTER SEVEN

CARRIE couldn't sleep. The heat of the night and the intense darkness seemed to be pressing down on her. She tossed and turned in the huge double bed trying not to think about Andreas—trying not to analyse too deeply the madness that had possessed her when they'd kissed! It was a moment best forgotten. She'd put it down to grief, to the fact that her brain wasn't operating properly—to anything other than the fact that she still wanted him...because that was too crazy to contemplate.

She didn't want to think about Jo and Theo either, because every time she did she wanted to cry. Or about Lilly, and what her life would be like growing up in a household where, primarily, people were paid to care about her.

Desperately Carrie tried to make her mind a blank so that the blissful oblivion of sleep would claim her. But the upsetting thoughts just kept going around and around.

At four o'clock she gave up the pretence of even trying to sleep and went to check on Lilly. The little girl was fast asleep, the night light in the corner sending a faint shimmer of gold over her. She was like a sleeping angel Carrie thought as she leaned over the cot to watch her.

She couldn't bear to think of her left here without a mother to care for her. Carrie knew the pain of that only too well!

Maybe she could take her home with her? The idea stole quietly into Carrie's mind from nowhere. At first she tried to dismiss it. Her job was so hectic; she probably did as much travelling around as Andreas.

But unlike Andreas she wasn't consumed by business. She could look for another job, she told herself feasibly, one that didn't take her away so much; she could even try and work from home as a financial consultant—that way she would be on hand to deal with Lilly's needs and schooling.

The idea started to grow on her.

The new job would have to be well paid, of course, because, apart from the fact that it cost a lot of money to bring a child up, she had one hell of a mortgage hanging around her neck. But maybe she could downsize? She couldn't go any smaller than her tiny one-bed flat, but it was located in a very prestigious area in the centre of London. She could move out to the country. And that would be a better life for Lilly anyway.

Carrie smiled to herself as she imagined them together. She'd get somewhere with a little garden, and put a swing there for Lilly to play on. She'd invite her school friends for tea and sleepovers. The two of them would be very happy. A little girl needed a mum.

And Andreas...? The question hovered in her mind for a moment, just the thought of his name making the turmoil inside her return. Well he could visit whenever he wanted, she supposed. He probably wouldn't want to come very often anyway; he would be too busy running his business empire.

Carrie smiled to herself, suddenly feeling a lot better than she had. The decision made, she reached over and kissed the sleeping baby before returning to bed and the bliss of sleep.

The sound of crying woke Carrie. It was still semi-dark; only a pink swirl of light lit the sky outside. She was disorientated for a moment before she remembered where she was and sprang quickly out of bed to see to the child.

Snapping up her dressing gown from next to the bed, she wrapped it around herself as she went into the nursery.

'There, there, what's the matter, sweetheart?' she murmured

as she bent over the cot. Lilly immediately stopped crying and smiled happily up at her.

'You little fraudster, what was all that noise about, hmm?' Carrie smiled and leaned in to stroke a hand over the side of her face.

'She probably needs a bottle and changing, but not necessarily in that order.'

The deep voice from behind her made Carrie whirl around in surprise.

Andreas was standing in the doorway, looking nonchalantly relaxed, and more handsome than any man had a right to be so early in the morning. He was dressed in a dark suit, a white shirt open at his neck.

'You startled me!' she murmured edgily, securing her dressing gown more tightly around her waist. 'What are you doing in here? What do you want?'

'What do you think I want?' One dark eyebrow rose. 'I'm simply checking that Lilly is OK.'

'Of course she's OK, she's with me,' Carrie muttered, her skin starting to burn with embarrassment as she noticed his gaze flicking down over the curves of her body and her long bare legs with a decidedly male interest.

'You've no right to come barging in here,' she said distractedly. 'You should have knocked.'

'I did knock, but you obviously didn't hear me.' He came further into the room and stopped next to her to look down into the cot. 'Good morning, Lilly…are you going to be a good girl today for Auntie Carrie?' He leaned in and tickled the child and she giggled happily.

'Did she sleep OK last night?' He looked back up towards Carrie and she nodded.

'Not a peep out of her.'

'I thought I didn't hear anything.'

'Well, you wouldn't, would you, from across the corridor?' Carrie wanted him to go; she was acutely self-conscious about her lack of clothing. Acutely aware that the last time she had been around him wearing a dressing gown he had felt free to slip his hand beneath the silk material...

'Believe me, after three sleepless weeks my ear is so highly tuned to listening out for Lilly that I'm sure I'd hear her cough from as far away as my office in Athens.' He smiled at Carrie.

She didn't like the way his smile affected her, didn't like the way his words immediately conjured up a loving uncle who would put his niece high on his lists of priorities! She'd made a decision last night. Lilly would be better off with her, and even though daylight was breaking outside she still felt strongly about that. This was no rash judgement but a sane resolution. Andreas was too busy with his business, he couldn't look after a baby, and she needed to talk to him about it sensibly and as soon as possible, without any of the craziness of yesterday blurring things.

'Anyway, I'd better go.' He glanced at his wristwatch. 'I've got a meeting at nine. I've jotted the telephone number of my office down for you. It's on the pad in my study along with my mobile number. Ring me if you have any problems.'

'Thanks, but I won't have any problems.'

'Good.' For a moment his eyes drifted distractedly over the tumble of her blonde hair and then down over her sensuous curves so tantalizingly close. And he found himself thinking about the way she had responded to him last night—found himself wanting to draw her closer, explore her reactions to him some more. Irritated by the thought, he glanced again at his watch. Business had to come first this morning; he had a board-room full of people to deal with.

He would deal with his need for Carrie later. 'Marcia will be here at nine-thirty. Meanwhile Lilly's routine is written down in the kitchen, if there is anything you are unsure of, or if you need a hand just ask Marcia when she arrives.'

The brisk businesslike tone was starting to irritate her; did he think she couldn't cope?

'Andreas, I can manage perfectly well.'

'If I didn't think that, I wouldn't be leaving Lilly with you,' he retorted firmly. 'I have no doubts that she is in a safe pair of hands.'

She smiled at him. Now this was exactly what she wanted to hear. 'You know, that's probably the nicest thing you've said to me since I arrived.'

'Is it?' There was a teasing gleam in his eye suddenly, one that sent delicious shivery sensations rushing through her. And she found herself thinking about the other things he had said…about how much they still wanted each other…

Urgently she tried to ignore all of that and concentrate on practicalities. 'I think we got off to a bad start yesterday.'

He smiled. 'I wouldn't put it in quite those terms.'

'We need to forget all that craziness, Andreas,' she told him quickly. 'And sit down and sort out what is the best thing for Lilly.'

'I've already sorted out what is best for Lilly. I start interviewing nannies tomorrow.' Andreas glanced at his watch again. 'I'm going to have to go.'

'Well, let's discuss this later, then,' Carrie suggested quickly. 'What time do you get home?'

'Six…no, maybe closer to seven. I have a lot on today.' He leaned into the cot to give Lilly a kiss. 'See you later, cutie.'

Lilly chuckled happily, making Carrie smile.

'Right, I'm out of here.' Andreas turned for the door.

'And we'll discuss things later, OK?' Carrie started to follow after him, but Lilly cried as she moved away.

Hastily Carrie returned to the cot and picked the little girl up. 'It's OK, honey. I haven't forgotten you.'

Lilly smiled at her, happy now.

'Let's go and say goodbye to Uncle Andreas, shall we? See if we can have a quick word about you.' She carried the child out through the bedroom and into the corridor. But Andreas was already halfway downstairs.

'Andreas, we do need to discuss Lilly,' she said as she followed him.

'There's nothing to discuss,' he murmured as he went across to pick up a tie that was sitting on top of his briefcase on the hall table. 'But you can be present at the interviews tomorrow if that will make you feel happier.'

'Thanks—but I don't think that's going to make any difference to how I feel about this situation.' She watched as he secured the pale blue tie with deft fingers.

'Well, there's not much else I can suggest.' He picked up his briefcase.

'But I have an idea.' She blurted the words out before he could disappear through the front door. 'Something that could really solve all problems.'

He turned and looked at her then. 'What kind of an idea?'

She hesitated. Part of her was so excited by her plan that she wanted to tell him right now—but another part of her knew that this needed careful handling. 'We'll talk about it later tonight, OK? I'll make us some dinner.' She made the offer impulsively. 'We'll sit down and forget all about the past between us and talk things through.'

One dark eyebrow rose. 'Is this the same woman who was hiding in her room from me last night?'

'I wasn't hiding! I told you—I was tired, that was all. I'd had a very long day and…' she lifted her chin up defiantly '—and anyway you behaved badly!'

'Did I indeed?' Andreas laughed and the sound made disconcerting little waves of awareness trickle through her bloodstream. 'Why, because I kissed you and you wanted me? Or because I didn't follow through?'

'I did not want you to kiss me! Or…anything else!'

'That wasn't what your eyes said…or what your kiss said…'

This conversation wasn't going in the direction she wanted it to at all! 'Let's just forget all about that, OK?' she asked desperately.

He smiled. 'Sweep it all under the carpet—pretend it didn't happen.'

'We'll talk about Lilly,' she told him firmly. 'At about seven-thirty tonight after I've put her down and got her settled.'

He shrugged. 'It's a date, then.'

'I wouldn't exactly put it like that!' she told him quickly.

'No, of course not.' He smiled.

He had the most gorgeous eyes, she thought distractedly. Come-to-bed eyes that could fire the blood with just a glance.

Why was she thinking about things like that? It definitely didn't help! 'We'll have a frank discussion,' she reiterated her intentions firmly. 'Put the past to bed.'

The words swirled between them, and Andreas raised a knowing eyebrow.

And suddenly her practical approach felt more like setting the scene for seduction.

'You know what I mean,' she murmured uncomfortably. 'Stop winding me up.'

He just looked amused and walked away.

The man was infuriating, she thought angrily as he closed the front door behind him. He seemed to get some kind of perverse enjoyment out of seeing her blush.

She could see him through the lattice glass as he walked past his car towards the helicopter that was sitting at the far side of the house. Curiously she crossed to the window to watch as he climbed into the machine. A few seconds later there was the roar of the engine and the whirl of the blades as it lifted up into the pale morning sky and headed out towards the sea.

When had Andreas obtained his pilot's licence? she wondered. She'd assumed when she saw the helicopter yesterday that he employed someone to fly him around. But piloting himself had to make getting backwards and forwards from work a lot quicker and easier.

However, it didn't change the fact that most of the time Andreas wouldn't be here, she reminded herself firmly. Talking to him tonight and getting full custody of Lilly was imperative.

Lilly stirred restlessly in her arms and she kissed the top of the child's head. 'Come on, let's go and get you ready for breakfast.'

Carrie didn't have much time to think about Andreas for the rest of the morning. It was amazing how absorbing it was looking after a small baby. Even when she had put Lilly down for her afternoon nap there were other tasks waiting. Lilly's clothing needed sorting out. Someone had obviously just emptied the wardrobes from her nursery at Jo and Theo's and then placed everything randomly back in drawers here. Consequently her clothes had become jumbled up, and there were a lot of things from a few weeks ago that no longer fitted her now.

Carrie sorted the old stuff out and put it into bags and Marcia said she'd ask around to see if anyone in the village wanted it.

Later in the afternoon, when Marcia had gone home, Carrie placed Lilly in her pram and took her for a walk. The day was filled with a languid heat and an overwhelming blue sky. They reached a secluded cove at the end of the lane and sat in the shade for a while enjoying the breeze that whispered in over the sea. Lilly looked adorable in her little white sunhat, and she had a great time throwing her teddy out of the pram so that Carrie could pick it up for her over and over again.

Her gurgling laughter was so infectious that Carrie found herself enjoying the game too. It wasn't until they headed for home that she realized that the evening was fast approaching and she hadn't even thought about what she was going to cook for dinner, let alone exactly what she was going to say to Andreas.

An investigation of the fridge revealed it was very well stocked. She found a joint of lamb and lots of fresh vegetables. And Marcia had told her earlier that there was a kitchen garden at the side of the house with every fresh herb imaginable.

The food taken care of, Carrie tried to concentrate on how best to tackle the subject of taking Lilly back to England as she bathed the little girl before bed.

Should she drop the suggestion in casually? Or go for a full on approach? The situation needed careful handling. After all this was Andreas's brother's child—and she knew that blood ties were important, that his Greek pride would not want to allow for the fact that Lilly would be better off with her.

But she *would* be better off with her, Carrie thought determinedly as she watched Lilly splashing in the water and laughing up at her.

A child needed a mother, needed a secure and stable environment, not a changing rotation of staff. Carrie needed to impress that point on Andreas, and she was sure he would see the sense of it. After all, he was a self-confessed workaholic.

But as darkness fell and Carrie tucked Lilly into her cot and kissed her goodnight nervous anticipation increased.

What if Andreas said no?

The thought was unbearable.

If he didn't give his consent she would have no choice but to accept his decision because she had no legal right to challenge him.

As it approached seven Carrie's nerves started to stretch to breaking point.

Dinner was under control and after careful consideration she had even set the table in the dining room—rather than the kitchen.

Now she was standing in her bedroom wondering what to wear.

Should she go for the little black dress that was understated yet sexy…or just a casual pair of cropped trousers and a T-shirt? What kind of look was required?

It couldn't hurt to look her best, she reasoned. A relaxing ambience might just ease the path, might make Andreas more receptive to what she had to say.

But then this wasn't about how she looked, this was about a serious decision that would affect the rest of Lilly's life! She rejected the dress and put on the capri trousers and T-shirt.

Then ten minutes before Andreas was due home she changed back into the dress and went downstairs. Every little helped.

She was preparing a Greek salad as a starter when she heard the sound of the helicopter coming in.

Hurriedly she went through her prepared speech for the millionth time.

I've given this a lot of thought, Andreas, and I really think...

She heard the front door open and then the sound of his footsteps down the hallway.

And I really think... Her mind seemed to go into some kind of weird freefall as he appeared in the doorway.

'Hi, how's it going?' He smiled.

'Just fine. How was your day?'

'Busy.' His gaze swept slowly over her before moving to the pans on the stove behind her. 'This is all very...domesticated.'

'Is it?' She tried to pretend she didn't notice the slight edge in his tone, and that she wasn't overly aware of everything about him as he leaned against the door and regarded her with those dark penetrating eyes.

'Well...I said I'd cook dinner—didn't I?'

'You did indeed. I just didn't expect you to be going to quite so much...trouble.'

She was very aware of his eyes flicking over her again, taking in everything about her appearance, from the high-heeled shoes to the little dress with the shoestring straps.

'You look lovely,' he told her.

'Thanks.'

Their eyes connected and there was a moment's tense silence between them. Carrie could feel herself heating up inside. Why was she so overly aware of him? she wondered angrily. She wanted this chemistry or whatever it was that was swirling in the air between them now to go away—it was complicating things far too much.

'So how was Lilly today?' he asked quietly.

'Good.' She nodded and wondered suddenly if she sounded monosyllabic. Her brain didn't seem to want to function; all she could think about was the strange feelings of yearning that he could stir up inside her. She shouldn't feel like this, she told herself angrily—Andreas meant nothing to her, whereas Lilly was all that mattered. 'She had a really good day,' she empha-sized briskly.

'I'm glad. You can tell me all about it when I come back downstairs. How long will dinner be?'

'About twenty minutes.'

Andreas nodded. 'I'll go say goodnight to her and then freshen up. Won't be long.'

'She's asleep. But take your time, it's all under control here.'

The longer he took, the more chance it gave her to rally herself, Carrie thought as she watched him head down the hallway.

She opened some bottled water and poured herself a glass before putting the rest in a jug to carry through to the dining room.

The table looked excellent, the crystalware and modern settings gleaming in the subdued lighting. Carrie flicked on another side lamp. She didn't want the place to look too intimate and to that end she resisted lighting the candles on the sideboard. She wanted a soothing and yet formal mood. It was important to keep things casual yet focused.

Now all she needed to do was make her case clearly.

For a moment she stood in the open doorway that led out to the patio. The night air was warm, the only sounds were the cicadas and the distant wash of the tide against the shore, the only light in the darkness was the warmth spilling out from the house and the distant neon blue of the swimming pool.

Was taking Lilly away from all of this really the right thing? The negative thought crept in before she could halt it. And, frowning, she pushed it away. The house was spectacular, and certainly much grander than anything she could provide for Lilly. But money and privilege didn't bring happiness. People were what counted. Being loved…feeling secure…those were the important things in life.

'You were right, she was fast asleep.' Andreas came into the room behind her and Carrie whirled around. He'd changed into black jeans and a white T-shirt that emphasized the powerful width of his shoulders. He looked relaxed and yet brimming with a kind of vital energy that made her senses go on high alert.

'No doubt she's growing another few inches.' She smiled.

'Yes. I'm going to have to try and get home a bit earlier from work in future so that I can see a bit more of her. Otherwise she will be all grown up before I know it.'

The affectionate concern in his words made Carrie feel uncomfortable and she tried to counter the feeling with the reminder that he was still planning on going to work every day—getting home an hour earlier wasn't going to help much in the grand scheme of looking after Lilly.

'Your work is very demanding.'

He shrugged. 'But never a problem until now.'

That wasn't how Carrie remembered it. In their short time together she'd constantly been aware of his business interests taking precedence. Obviously it hadn't bothered him back then, because he hadn't cared enough about her for it to matter. At least he cared about Lilly enough to realize it now needed addressing. And hopefully that would work in her favour for custody, she thought anxiously.

'We'll talk about it over dinner. Why don't you sit down and I'll get our food?' she suggested.

To her consternation Andreas didn't do as she asked, but followed her through to the kitchen again and watched as she organized the aperitifs.

To some extent her domesticity amused him. He knew damn well that she was up to something. She probably couldn't cook. Like him, she probably ate the majority of meals in sophisticated restaurants in the city after work. Before Lilly had arrived that was how Andreas had liked to live his life. The majority of his meals had been eaten out, relationships at a distance, nothing too cosy for comfort. It was easier to keep himself emotionally separate when he conducted affairs like that.

However, he found the experience of watching Carrie

working in his kitchen curiously fascinating. Whatever she was up to, she looked damn sexy.

Conscious of his eyes following her as she bent down at the cooker, she flicked a glance over at him and he smiled.

'So what's for dinner?' he asked lazily.

She wished he wouldn't look at her like that; it was as if he were undressing her with his eyes. Trying hard not to let him affect her, she started to detail the menu, talking quickly, trying to cover how nervous he was making her.

'I didn't realize you were such a domestic goddess.'

The dry mocking tone grated on her. 'I'm not!'

Andreas watched the way her hair slid silkily around her bare shoulders as she pushed it out of the way to glance over at him.

She was one sexy piece of work, he thought distractedly. From time to time during his meetings today thoughts of her had encroached...clouding his mind with need.

What was she up to? His gaze moved slowly over the little black dress, noting how it clung lovingly to her slender curves. Why was she so keen to talk to him that she was cooking up a storm in his kitchen, flicking those wide blue eyes so provocatively at him?

'However, Andreas, I am more than capable of producing good home-cooked food,' she told him hastily, mindful that she needed to impress upon him her credentials for bringing Lilly up well.

'Is that so?'

'Absolutely.' Her heart started to thud uneasily against her chest. He still sounded as if he was mocking her. She returned her attention swiftly to the aperitifs. 'And everything is done now, so let's move through to the other room.'

'I think, before that, you should tell me exactly what's really on your mind, Carrie.'

The quiet words made her almost drop the side plates she had taken out of the cupboard. 'How do you mean?' She hedged for time as she glanced over at him. She didn't want to just launch coldly into talking about Lilly; she wanted him to be sitting comfortably, and she wanted him to unwind so that he could really think about what she was saying.

'Well, let's put it another way. Precisely why are you trying to impress me with this new found domesticity?'

The question made Carrie's skin flood with colour. 'It's not new—I like cooking! I just don't get time to do it much at home. And I'm not trying to impress you!' Her voice rose slightly. 'I told you this morning. We need to relax, and talk frankly about things—and what better way than over a good meal?'

'The way to a man's heart is through his stomach and all that?' His lips twisted. 'Is that what you mean?'

There it was again, the derisive mocking tone.

'No, it is not!' Her voice was low, like a whispered plea. 'This isn't about us. This is about Lilly.'

He nodded, but the darkness of his eyes didn't waver from hers. 'So tell me what it is you want and let's get it over with.'

There was a hard edge to his voice that made her want to avoid the question completely—but she knew now that she couldn't. Andreas was too shrewd to be fobbed off. All she could do was throw herself at his mercy.

So she placed the side plates down on the edge of the counter, and turned to face him.

'OK, but before I tell you, I want you to promise me that you will think about this very carefully. We need to put Lilly first, above everything…above you, me…shadows of the past…*everything*.'

'You've got no argument there—that's exactly what I am doing—so please do go on. You have my full attention, I assure you.'

She swallowed hard, really not liking that smooth yet incredibly steely tone.

'I think you should give me custody of Lilly.'

CHAPTER EIGHT

THERE, it was out.

For a second there was a look of surprise on his handsome features and then to her consternation he just laughed.

'Not a hope in hell, Carrie.'

'But you haven't even thought about it!' Her breath caught. 'Please Andreas…I'm…I'm begging you.'

'Are you indeed?' His eyes swept over her, noting how beautiful she looked at that moment, how incredibly bright blue her eyes were, how her skin was flushed, her lips parted.

'So you've gone to all this trouble—cooked for me, dressed up for me—so you can take Lilly back to London?'

'I didn't dress up for you!' The grating sarcasm tore into her. 'I just wanted to make an effort so we could relax and talk about this properly. I honestly think it would be the best thing for her, Andreas. You can't look after a baby. Your work comes first, it always has!'

'On the contrary, Carrie, business used to come first. But now my niece comes first.'

'So, are you going to give everything up for her?' she countered, her voice shaking with emotion. 'Are you going to dedicate yourself entirely to making a home for her instead of rushing off to the office every day, leaving her to the mercy of strangers?'

'The mercy of strangers?' His eyes narrowed. 'That's a very

dramatic way of putting it! I'm going to employ somebody professional to help me look after her. It's what a lot of working
parents do.'

'She doesn't need a professional! She's a little girl—she
needs a mother!' The words broke from her lips painfully and
her eyes glistened with unshed tears. Impatiently she moved to
brush them away and her arm caught the plates next to her, dis-
lodging them, sending them smashing down onto the tiled floor.

The sound matched the way Carrie was feeling. 'Now look
what I've done! I knew we should have discussed this calmly
sitting down over dinner!' Embarrassed, she bent to clear the
mess up. Emotional outbursts weren't going to help her case, she
told herself firmly. Andreas was a hard-headed businessman—
she needed to appeal to that cool, pragmatic side of him. Trouble
was she didn't feel cool or pragmatic right now. She couldn't
even see what she was doing, her eyes were so misted with tears.

Everything had gone hopelessly wrong! Andreas wasn't
even considering her words. What chance was there now for
being able to support Lilly and love her?

Andreas watched as she tried to pick up the jagged pieces
of crockery, noting her angry, jerky movements.

'You are going to hurt yourself, Carrie.' He stood where he
was for a moment before coming to help her. 'Leave it—I'll
get a brush.'

But it was too late; she'd already caught her wrist on a sharp
edge, and bright droplets of blood trickled onto the floor.

He followed her towards the sink as she rinsed the wound
and he found the first-aid box for her in a drawer.

'Do you need some help?'

'No, thanks, I can manage.' She flicked him an angry look.
'All I want from you is for you to please just think about my
suggestion for Lilly.'

He didn't reply, just watched as she struggled to find some
plasters and some antiseptic in the box.

'Andreas?'

'Let me look at that.' Before she could stop him he had taken hold of her arm and turned her around towards him.

His manner was resolved, his expression rigid and she had little choice but to allow him to take over. But the touch of his hand against her skin inflamed her senses even more, his closeness making her feel even more helpless...

'Andreas, will you please at least think about what I'm suggesting?' She tried again.

He drenched the cut on her hand with the antiseptic and it stung like crazy. 'Ouch! That hurts!' She tried to pull away.

'Carrie, just keep still! Hell, but you're a bad patient!'

'Well, you're a lousy doctor!'

She winced and glanced down. The gash was deeper than she had first thought and it was still pumping blood. He applied some firm pressure with a wad of lint and after a while the bleeding stopped.

'There, that's better.'

'Thanks.' She murmured the word reluctantly as he deftly wrapped a bandage over the area.

'You're welcome.'

For a second their eyes held. He was too close; she could see the gold flecks in the darkness of his eyes, the faint shadow of stubble on the firm line of his jaw, the sensual curve of his lips.

She could feel her heartbeats starting to increase. Hastily she moved back a step, trying to break whatever spell it was that seemed to hit whenever he was nearby. 'But I could have managed by myself!' she added uneasily.

He smiled. 'Hard to manage single-handedly.'

'Yes, and you'll find that out very quickly when you're juggling a baby and a newspaper empire,' she retorted.

'It may have escaped your notice, Carrie, but I'm already doing that.' He started to put everything away in the first-aid box again.

'And you're already having difficulties. From what you've told me you've hardly been able to do any work over the last couple of weeks.'

'Things will get better once I employ someone full time.'

'Andreas, a little girl needs a mother,' she implored softly. 'Think about it.'

He put the box back on the shelf and glanced over at her, noting how pale she looked, how her eyes still shimmered with feeling.

'So, you've looked after Lilly for one day and you suddenly think you've got what it takes to look after a child full time and be a mother?'

The condescending tone hurt.

'I *know* I have.' She held his gaze determinedly. 'I understand your reservations, but this isn't just a whim, Andreas, I promise you. I love Lilly, I have from the moment Jo placed her into my arms six months ago.'

'And what about your work?' he asked. 'Jo told me you have a very demanding job, and that you travel all over the world.'

'Yes, but—'

'Working for a bank, is that right?'

'Does it matter?' She shrugged, impatient to get on with what was important.

'Of course it matters. You've just asked me to hand over my niece to you—do you think I'm going to do that without question?'

Was he reconsidering? Hope sprang up inside her. 'OK, well, yes, I do travel, my current remit is preventing fraud in the banking system, but I—'

'So how often are you away from London?' he cut across her.

'It varies. Sometimes I'm away all month, sometimes for a few days, but if I had custody of Lilly I—'

'So what exactly is the difference between you and I…hmm? What makes you think that Lilly would be any better off with you?'

'I can't believe you've even had to ask that question!' she retaliated swiftly. 'The difference between us is clear—business doesn't come first with me. It isn't my whole existence!'

'It was when you left here two years ago.'

Their eyes met in a fierce clash that sent resounding waves of disturbance through her. 'That was different…'

'Was it?' He shrugged, then held up a hand. 'Hey, you don't need to make excuses to me, Carrie, for putting work first. I've been doing it for years.'

'I'm not making excuses! This is about a child! Something much more important than anything between us.'

Her dismissive tone stirred his anger and the words swirled inside him with raw emphasis. 'I know about the overwhelming importance of a child, Carrie.'

'So will you reconsider my idea?' She looked up at him anxiously, but it was hard to tell what he was thinking, his features were closed, yet the burning intensity of his eyes didn't leave hers.

'I'll give up my job, Andreas, and get another one working from home, so that I won't be travelling away,' she continued hurriedly. 'I'll put Lilly absolutely first in my life—above everything. I was thinking last night that I could sell my flat and buy something in the country, somewhere that would be handy for schools etcetera—'

'You've got everything figured out, haven't you?'

There was a cold kind of anger in that question that made her very uneasy.

'Not really, that's why I wanted us to sit down and talk.' She swallowed. 'Look, if you're worried that by giving me custody it means you won't have any say in Lilly's life then you needn't be! I want you to be involved. And you can come and see her whenever you want—I think it's important that you play a part in her life.'

One dark eyebrow rose mockingly. 'That's very big of you. How much of a part are you thinking of allowing me? Perhaps I can fly to London for an hour on a Saturday once a month, or maybe you just want me to send a cheque?'

'No, I do not! This isn't about money, Andreas!'

'Isn't it? Whether you like it or not, it is a realistic fact that money is needed to bring up a child.'

'And I will manage very well. I'm highly qualified and—

'And what about this guy you're seeing in London?' Andreas swept across her words with disdain. 'How does he figure in all this?'

There was silence. Carrie didn't know whom he was talking about for a moment, and she nearly asked, *What guy?* Then she remembered her lie last night about Mike and bit down hard on her lip. Why had she said something so stupid? Should she confess right now that she had just conjured him up in an instinctively defensive reaction? Tell him that the relationship was in the past? Admitting to a lie didn't sound too good when she was trying to convince him that she was of good enough character to take care of Lilly.

'Carrie?' His eyes were searing into her now. 'Are you going to answer my question?'

'Of course I'm going to answer.' Her cheeks flushed a bright uncomfortable pink. 'He doesn't figure in this at all,' she admitted huskily.

'No?' He watched her sceptically. He'd noted her hesitation—he'd learnt to read people well enough to know she wasn't telling him the whole truth. 'So what happened? Did you run this by him before you got here, and find out that he's a nice guy but not nice enough to take on someone else's child?'

Carrie didn't like the mockery in that question. 'Let's just leave Mike out of this, shall we?'

'Have I hit a raw nerve?'

'No! But right now this only concerns Lilly, you and I.'

He shook his head. 'Actually, Carrie, if we are going to be pedantic, this has absolutely nothing to do with you at all.'

The coldness of his words struck her like a physical blow; he could see her flinch, see the colour draining from her face. But Andreas found himself watching her reaction imperviously.

'How can you say that?' she whispered. 'When you know how much she means to me?'

'Because she's my brother's child, Theo appointed me her legal guardian and she belongs here with me in my home and in my country. She will be brought up with all the traditions and the love and respect that go with that.'

'So when you were asking me all those questions just now about my job and my plans—you really had no intention of changing your mind?'

'None whatsoever.' He shrugged. 'I was just curious as to how your mind is running.'

'You really are completely heartless, aren't you?' She flung the words at him furiously.

'Probably…' He reached out and tipped her chin up so that he could look at her and the gentle touch of his hand against her skin made her senses swirl with confusion. 'But where Lilly is concerned I am acting out of love…I want the best for her.'

The huskiness of those words opened an ache inside her that she couldn't begin to fathom.

She pulled away from him sharply.

She didn't doubt that Andreas loved Lilly; it was there in the way he looked at the child, the way he talked about her.

'Then think about what I've said!' she implored. 'You can't abandon her to be brought up by staff!'

'I have no intention of abandoning her, Carrie, and I resent the accusation. But I can't walk away from my business. It just isn't feasible right now. There are a lot of jobs and a lot of people depending on me—Lilly being the most important one.'

'Well, you obviously haven't thought the situation through! A nanny will only stay for as long as it suits her and then she will move on to the next job, or leave to have children of her own. That will cause Lilly to face another loss in her life and that situation could be repeated again and again.'

'Whereas with you she will just have to deal with a changing rotation of boyfriends who come and go—but that's OK, is it?' he grated.

'I wouldn't allow that to be a problem.'

'So what are you going to do about it? Become a nun for the rest of your life?'

The facetious comment really infuriated her. 'I will do whatever it takes, Andreas! Anything to make Lilly's life more secure,' she flared immediately.

'Anything?' He leaned back against the counter and surveyed her lazily from the tip of her high heels up over her long legs and sensuous body to linger on her flushed countenance. 'Somehow I don't think the nun's habit would suit you, Carrie. Maybe you need to rethink that.'

'Joke all you want—' she tipped her head up defiantly '—but I am prepared to put Lilly first and dedicate myself entirely to bringing her up. Whereas you—in your usual cold, clinical, businesslike style—are just going to use your wealth to buy her the kind of lifestyle you think she needs.'

'Actually, I'm going to buy her the kind of lifestyle that I *know* she needs,' he corrected her calmly. 'And luckily I can afford the very best of everything for her.'

'Well, good for you! But at the end of the day it's still going to be the staff who tucks Lilly into bed while you're tied up with the business.'

He held her gaze. 'Not if I take a wife.'

The cool comment completely threw Carrie and for a few stunned moments all she could do was stare at him in astonishment. 'A wife?'

'Why not?' He shrugged. 'It's a realistic solution to the problem.'

'But…you told me that you would never get married. I remember you said categorically that it just—how was it you put it?—it just *wasn't you*.' Her voice wasn't quite steady.

'Well, my situation has changed, hasn't it? I have Lilly to consider now. And, as you have already so eloquently pointed out, I need to put her needs first.'

Carrie was struck speechless for what felt like an eternity and when she finally found her voice it didn't even sound as if it belonged to her.

'And you would marry simply for Lilly?'

'Why not?' He regarded her coolly.

Carrie hadn't expected this! All her plans, all her solutions were worthless next to this. And she didn't doubt that Andreas would find himself a suitable wife—women would be queuing around the block for him. Maybe he even had someone in mind? Perhaps someone he was dating right now? She imagined a stunningly beautiful sophisticated woman…probably Greek… Yes, ultimately Andreas would probably choose a Greek woman to be his bride and bring Lilly up.

She wasn't prepared for the way that made her feel. It was as if a void had opened up inside her and it hurt. Desperately she tried to look at it in a positive light. It would be better for Lilly.

But it was hard to stifle the sudden feeling of resentment towards this unknown woman whom she was losing out to. Jealousy wasn't an emotion she was acquainted with, but she could feel it now, ugly and intensely real.

Carrie tried to tell herself that it was a natural reaction. Lilly was the closest thing to family she had left…and when Andreas took a wife there was a possibility that she would be squeezed out of the child's life. *And it would mean losing Andreas all over again too…*

The added disquieting thought made her frown. Andreas had never been hers to lose, she reminded herself. He'd never told her he loved her—*he'd never even made love to her*. All they had was this chemistry…a kind of friction that frankly she didn't understand. So why should she feel as if she were losing him? She had no right to think that way even for a moment.

Her eyes lifted to his. 'So have you got someone in mind?' She forced herself to continue the conversation.

Andreas could see that she was visibly shaken. She had been so passionate and emphatic in her plea for custody that she probably hadn't thought for one moment that he would produce this solution.

Had she really thought that he would just let her waltz off with his niece—his flesh and blood? That he would allow her to persuade this guy she was seeing in London to play happy families with her? Did she think for one moment that he could bear for her to do that?

The fury and rawness of that thought stirred up a grim determination inside him.

'I have, as a matter of fact.'

Carrie nodded. 'I hope you'll make sure it's someone who will bond with Lilly—someone who cares deeply about her.'

'That goes without saying.'

'You won't shut me out of her life, will you, Andreas?'

There were deep shadows in her violet-blue eyes, and her skin was so pale it was almost translucent.

But he was unmoved by her distress. The way she had set out to get Lilly by using any weapons at her disposal, even her femininity, galled him. The way she had spoken so dismissively about his commitment towards his niece infuriated him. His love for Lilly wasn't up for question—how dared she?

No, if Carrie wanted to be in Lilly's life it would be on his terms—he would have what he wanted out of this deal.

'That depends on you, Carrie,' he told her coldly.

'In what way?' She looked up at him her brow furrowed, a worried light in her clear blue eyes.

'There's only one way I would contemplate sharing custody of Lilly with you—and that's if you apply for the position of my wife yourself.'

For a moment she thought she had heard him wrong. 'I don't understand, Andreas…'

'I think you do.' He met her eyes coldly. 'You've just told me in very lofty noble terms how you are prepared to put Lilly first. Well, great—that makes you just the woman I need. Now prove your sincerity. Give your job up, stay here and be a mother to her. Give her the secure family life that you are so emphatically pleading for.'

CHAPTER NINE

'BY MARRYING you?' Carrie felt her voice sticking in her throat. She couldn't quite believe what she was hearing.

'Exactly.'

She waited for him to say something more, but he didn't. And the darkness of his gaze on hers was cold and uncompromising.

There was a part of her that wanted him to soften the offer, to wrap it up in more palatable terms, to pretend that he had some feeling for her—OK, not love, she corrected herself fiercely, because if he suddenly declared that he loved her it would be an obvious lie. But some kind of romantic spin on the proposition would have made it at least a little more…acceptable.

But the minutes ticked by and Andreas made no attempt to persuade her with soft words. Indeed he looked so stern and ruthless that Carrie felt even more out of her depth.

'So…are you suggesting a kind of business arrangement?' she ventured. 'A marriage in name only?'

The coldness of his expression was now replaced by a mocking gleam in the darkness of his eyes, a sardonic curl of his lips. 'Come on, Carrie—get real! You think I'm going to marry you and not take you to bed? My life may be dominated by business but I'm a red-blooded male.'

He watched the way the pallor of her skin scorched with fire. 'Let me spell it out for you,' he continued with brutal candour.

'I would expect you to play the part of devoted mother and very sexy wife to absolute perfection.'

The words caused a fierce consternation inside her, because, although she hated his cool detachment from any emotion, there was also a secret part of her that felt a wild excitement at the thought of giving herself up to him. Of being a mother to Lilly—of being a part of a family by day and by night allowing him to pleasure her, allowing those hands, those lips, to move freely over her body. She had spent so long in the past dreaming about it—speculating about it…

She looked away from him abruptly, ashamed of the sudden yearning he had stirred inside her. What he was suggesting was a shameless, loveless union, for heaven's sake. Where was her pride?

He placed a hand under her chin, forcing her to look up at him, not allowing her to evade the intensity of his gaze. 'So what do you say?'

Even the firm, uncompromising touch of his fingers against her skin was turning her on! She swallowed hard, hating herself. 'I think it is a—a barbaric idea!'

The fact that for a moment he had seen desire in her eyes and now she was trying to hide it—pretend it didn't exist— infuriated Andreas even more. She'd tried to do this last night as well—and it reminded him of the way she had walked out of his life the first time.

It also reminded him of a past relationship, one he preferred not to dwell on.

He dropped his hand from her skin. 'So go home to your safe little existence in London and let me get on with the job of bringing Lilly up.'

The derisive words twisted inside her. 'In other words if I don't agree to your…proposition, then effectively I will lose Lilly completely?'

'I would think that more or less sums up the situation.' He held her eyes coldly. 'As you so rightly pointed out, Lilly needs stability—she needs a mother. If you choose to go back to London, then that person is not you. You can't just flit in and out of her life when it suits you.'

'I know that!'

'Then if you are serious about your intentions towards Lilly you will realize that my proposition is the most sensible one.'

'But we don't love each other!' The words broke from her lips in a throaty whisper of distress.

For a moment his eyes held with hers and she could see a blaze of light burning in their depths, could see a pulse beating at the side of his strong jaw. 'This has nothing to do with love, Carrie—this has to do with practicalities.'

The words were so icy they took her breath away.

'But…for us to make a lifetime commitment—tie ourselves together as man and wife, share a bed, for heaven's sake…' Her voice trailed away as she saw his lips curve in a mocking smile.

'You think we need to love each other to share a bed—to enjoy ourselves?' He watched the bright glow of colour creep up under her skin at that question. 'Come along, Carrie, you are not the naïve young woman you were when we first met—surely?'

The words were so scathing that she felt foolish in the extreme.

'You're not still weighing relationships up, dreaming of an old-fashioned yet perfect liaison?' he continued.

'I have never dreamt of any such thing!' She angled her chin up. 'But don't you dare mock me, Andreas!' she continued furiously. 'There's nothing wrong in having ideals, or of thinking a relationship through sensibly! I know what real life is like. I know all about heartbreak. I watched my parents' marriage disintegrate, heard my mother cry herself to sleep every night when my father walked out.'

'Then you'll know that love is no magic guarantee for happy ever afters.'

She shrugged. 'What I know is that I don't want that kind of life—for me or for Lilly.'

'And do you think that this guy in London can offer you the

kind of security you crave?' Andreas grated. 'Because let me tell you—no matter what he has whispered in your ear when you make love, he can't have meant it otherwise he would have come to Pyrena with you, would have wanted to help you and be involved with Lilly.'

'Just leave Mike out of this, Andreas! You must know that I would never choose a man over Lilly. She is my goddaughter and I love her. She is and always will be my priority,' she snapped uncomfortably.

Andreas was privately relieved that Carrie seemed so willing to sacrifice her relationship with this Mike. He felt supremely confident that she would choose the life he offered her above all else.

'So, you see, I'm being realistic. Love is about compromise—nothing is perfect.'

'Well, our union sure as hell wouldn't be!'

'And that's something we'd have to work at, Carrie.' His eyes moved over her face, lingered on her lips and she started to feel hot inside with a different kind of emotion, one she didn't want to acknowledge at all.

'And we have one very real, very basic thing in our favour,' he murmured. 'The chemistry is right between us. We may not be in love but we sure as hell want each other.'

Carrie started to shake her head.

'You still don't want to believe that…hmm?' He reached out to take hold of her arm bringing her firmly in towards him. 'Let me remind you,' he grated huskily.

'Andreas, don't, I—'

Her words were cut off as his lips covered hers and instantly warmth and longing flooded through her entire body. Instinctively she responded, opening her mouth for him, her whole being pulsating with pleasure. His hands moved to cup her waist, at the same time bringing her in tightly against him. She could feel the hardness of his body pressing against her and it made her senses swirl with a need that was both primitive and raw. She wanted him—wanted him so much that her body was crying out to be even closer, for him to touch her more intimately.

His lips ravished the delicate softness of her mouth before trailing a heated path towards her neck, and she groaned with pleasure when at the same time his hands swept upwards over her body, finding her breasts, stroking roughly over the silk of her dress.

'You see, you like that...hmm?' He whispered the words against her ear as his fingers found the hard aroused peaks through the soft material, caressing over them so that they tightened even more into tight buds of excitement that throbbed for his touch. And suddenly she ached for him to pull the flimsy barrier of material away and possess her completely.

'You see I am right.' His voice rasped against her skin as his lips trailed a heated blaze down her neck. 'You want more, don't you? You want me to take you...satisfy you completely?'

'Yes...' She pressed closer in a complete delirium of need, almost unaware that she had answered. All she could think about was the craving he was stirring up inside her, a basic instinct as old as time that had overtaken everything else including pride and reserve.

He moved his hands from the warmth of her breast and unzipped her dress, pulling it down part way, exposing the creamy flesh to his ruthless gaze.

But then instead of continuing to caress her, kiss her, make love to her, he stepped back to look at her.

'Now what were you saying about desire not being a strong enough emotion?' He murmured the words softly, his eyes slowly ravishing her sultry pouting lips before moving down over the firm thrusting curve of her breasts in the lacy black bra. 'You want me in every sense of the word, Carrie,' he rasped as he watched the heated colour climb over the honey smoothness of her skin. 'You want me so much that if I were to continue caressing you now you would beg me to make love to you.'

Reality flooded in on the hazy world of longing that had somehow swept her away and she realized with horror that he had been kissing her merely to prove his point. Ashamed that he had succeeded so easily she pulled her dress back up over her curves with hands that trembled so much that she didn't dare to even attempt to zip herself up again.

'OK, you can turn me on!' Her eyes blazed with fury into his. 'But it doesn't mean anything—it's just a chemical reaction.'

'Call it what you want.' His gaze was hooded and dangerous. 'Frankly I don't give a damn. All I care about is the fact that we could make a relationship work, for Lilly's sake.'

It was astounding how he could kiss her with such passion yet sound so totally indifferent towards her. But then, as he had already pointed out long ago, love and desire were two very different things.

'Lust can't sustain a relationship,' she murmured distraughtly.

'But it helps. If there was no desire between us I wouldn't be suggesting this arrangement for one minute. Similarly if I didn't believe that you truly loved Lilly and would make a good mother for her, I would tell you to walk away.'

He noted how her hands shook as she zipped her dress back into place.

'You were the one who said you'd do anything to make Lilly's life more secure,' he reminded her gently.

'And I meant it!' She looked up at him, her eyes wide and filled with a glistening vulnerability that tore at him. 'But this…' She shook her head. 'This scares me, Andreas…'

He nodded and was suddenly fiercely glad that he had fought against the desire raging through him a few moments ago. Carrie needed to come to him…

'I understand.'

'You do?'

'Of course, this is a big step for both of us. But think about it—you and I could be the family Lilly so desperately needs.'

The words tore through her defences.

'Carrie, I will do my best to make both of you happy and secure.' He shrugged. 'I can say no more than that.'

Her heart ached as she looked up at him.

'Take some time and think about it,' he told her softly. 'For Lilly's sake I think it is the only way forward.'

Carrie tossed and turned in the large double bed. The heat of the night was intense. She couldn't sleep; the evening kept playing over and over in her mind, Andreas's proposal taunting her, mocking her, his words running through her like an instrument of torture.

Love is no magic guarantee for happy ever afters.

He was right: love hadn't held her parents' marriage together and they had been head over heels about each other when they'd walked down the aisle.

And Mike had told her he loved her, but it hadn't meant anything. He'd been lying to her, paying lip service to emotions he didn't feel just to get her into bed. When she'd found out he was seeing someone else he'd just shrugged. Said it was her fault for not sleeping with him.

At least Andreas was honest about his feelings. He'd never pretended to love her, never said the right words just to get her into bed.

And she did desire him… She remembered the heat of his kisses, and the way her body still responded to him with such intensity of passion. But it scared her that he could take such control over her senses, she'd always sworn that she would be careful about who she gave that power to.

Just walking away from Andreas two years ago had been unbelievably painful—so if she married him and it went wrong she didn't even dare speculate how that would feel. All she knew was that it would be devastating.

So what should she do?

Marrying Andreas would provide Lilly with the stability of a family. And surely that was the most important thing?

If she said no and walked away, then effectively she would be leaving Lilly to the mercy of staff on a regular basis—or to a stepmother who might resent her…

Really she had no choice but to accept Andreas's offer.

Carrie turned her pillow over trying to find a cool place so that she could think rationally.

Her mind drifted back to those moments in the kitchen when Andreas had told her to think over his proposition.

One moment he had been ruthlessly insistent, the next coolly pragmatic. He had turned his attention away from her towards the meal she had prepared. Had talked in general terms about Lilly as he had taken over the cooking and suggested moving through towards the dining room to relax.

Carrie hadn't wanted to eat anything and she'd felt as though she would never relax again, but somehow she had managed to gather herself together enough to sit opposite him at the dining table and had tried to act as nonchalantly and non-committally as he.

But inside her emotions had been swirling in confusion, just as they were now.

The pale pink of dawn was breaking outside and Lilly stirred in her cot. Carrie could hear her gurgling contentedly and the sound made her smile. Flinging back the covers, she reached for her dressing gown and went to see to her.

'Hello, darling—how are you today?' she murmured and the child smiled in delight and lifted her arms to be picked up.

'Are you hungry, honey?' Carrie reached in and lifted her.

How could she leave this little girl? The question twisted painfully inside her as she carried the child through the silence of the house and downstairs to make her a bottle.

How could she go back to her job in London and not be haunted by her day and night? Not worry about her—not fret about who was taking care of her?

She glanced out of the side window in the kitchen as she waited for the kettle to boil and saw Andreas swimming in the pool. He was cutting through the silky water with strong, firm strokes, going backwards and forwards without any breaks. His strength and energy held her spellbound for a few moments. Then as she watched he heaved himself out onto the side in one lithe movement. The gold light of early dawn played over the strength of his muscles.

He had a fabulous physique, lean and hard, not an ounce of spare flesh; she watched how his muscles rippled powerfully as he reached for a towel and something inside her turned over. Swiftly she averted her eyes trying to ignore the feeling—trying to tell herself that it meant nothing.

But as she placed the bottle in to heat for Lilly she couldn't resist looking out again. He was walking towards the kitchen door now just wearing a pair of low-slung jeans, a towel strung around his neck, his torso bare. He made a very striking picture against the gold blaze of sunflowers in the back field, his dark tanned body still glistening with water, his hair wet and slicked back from the hard boned aristocratic face.

'Morning, Carrie.' He swept in through the back door and smiled at her. 'Are you making coffee by any chance?'

His laid-back manner made her wonder if she had imagined his proposal last night—imagined the way he had made her feel as he had taken her into his arms.

'Er…yes—I've just boiled the kettle.' She tried desperately to match his tone. 'I'll make you some.'

'Thanks.' He crouched down next to Lilly's high chair. 'And how is my little sweetheart this morning?'

The words caused the strange aching feelings inside Carrie to intensify. She tried not to look over as Lilly laughed and gurgled up at him.

'Are you getting ready to go to the office?' she asked him.

'Not today, it's Saturday.'

'Is it? I'm losing track of time,' she murmured.

He turned his attention to her as she moved about the kitchen taking cups from the cupboards. He noticed how her blonde hair was silkily dishevelled, how her skin seemed pale, and her eyes too blue, too large for her face as she flicked a glance nervously over at him.

She had bare feet, he noticed, and the silk gown was tightly fastened around her curves.

'So what are your plans for today?' she asked as she put the coffee down on the table beside him.

'Interviews at nine, then the rest of the day is free. Do you want to sit in on them with me?'

He was still going ahead with interviewing staff, as if the proposal last night had never happened! The fact shouldn't have surprised her; after all, she hadn't given him an answer and the interviews were already arranged. But even so she felt tension escalate inside her.

Somehow she managed to nod. 'Yes…I will, thank you.' She took Lilly out of her high chair and sat down at the breakfast bar to give her the bottle she had prepared. The child suckled noisily and happily, looking up at Carrie with wide trusting eyes.

'She seems more settled since you arrived,' Andreas remarked as he watched her.

For a second their eyes connected and then before Carrie could gather herself together to make a reply he picked up his coffee and walked towards the door. 'I'm going to grab a shower. I'll see you down here a little later.'

By the time Carrie had dressed Lilly and then herself and returned downstairs, Marcia had arrived and the first of the candidates was waiting in the front reception room.

Carrie felt a pang of consternation as she stood with Lilly in her arms and glanced through the open doorway; the woman seemed younger than she had anticipated. She only looked sixteen or seventeen, her dark hair in plaits; she was dressed in a miniskirt with leggings and high heels.

'Has she got experience and a reference?' Carrie asked Andreas without preamble when she found him in his study.

'Of course.' He looked up and smiled at her. 'Relax—she wouldn't have made it to an interview otherwise.'

He pulled out the spare chair that had been placed beside him. 'Have a quick flick through the references before I call her in,' he invited as he slid a pile of papers over. 'We have three candidates and they all seem accomplished, experienced and are recommended by a highly reputable agency.'

Carrie sat down and tried to feel enthusiastic as she settled Lilly on her knee and reached for the papers.

An hour later and she felt the thin veil of enthusiasm slipping away. The first candidate, although young, seemed the best— at least she showed interest in Lilly when she came into the room, and she seemed genuinely sympathetic about her circumstances. But then it transpired that she would only be available to work for the next six months to a year as she was getting married and moving away.

The second candidate was an older woman with a stern, unsmiling countenance who hardly glanced at Lilly and seemed more interested in dictating her own terms.

Andreas cut her short after a while and they moved on to the third candidate, who couldn't speak a word of English so Carrie really didn't know what to think of her except that she only glanced at Lilly once on entering the room and then it was only to give her the barest of smiles.

Carrie felt completely stressed by the end of the proceedings. All she could imagine was Jo's face, and her gut instinct was telling her that her friend wouldn't have approved of any of these women as a full-time carer for Lilly.

'So what did you think?' Andreas asked as he got up to pour himself a coffee from the pot Marcia had left on the sideboard.

'I didn't think any of them were suitable,' Carrie said directly.

'Really?' Andreas frowned. 'I thought number three myself. Ms Koleumdoposis was easily the most suitable.'

'You're not serious!' Carrie stared at him in consternation.

'She only glanced at Lilly once, she didn't look in the slightest bit maternal…or even interested in her.'

'Well, in fairness you didn't understand what she was saying.' Andreas shrugged. 'She seemed pleasant enough.'

'Pleasant!' Carrie glared at him and then as Lilly fidgeted in her arms she stood up and placed her into the pram by the side of her. 'Pleasant isn't sufficient—pleasant doesn't cut it, Andreas!'

'Carrie, we can't expect someone who comes to work for us to be as besotted by Lilly as we are.' He shrugged. 'The best we can hope for is someone kind and reliable and I think Ms Koleumdoposis is that person. I would have gone for the first candidate only she's not going to stay and, as you said, we don't really want Lilly going through the trauma of changing staff. She needs routine and stability.'

'Andreas, you can't really be seriously thinking of leaving Lilly with that woman full time. I won't allow it—I won't condone it.'

Andreas looked over at her, a frown marring his handsome face. 'Carrie, I'm politely asking for your opinion, but that is as far as it goes.'

The steely words brought her back to reality with a thud. Of course she had no right to be so adamant. 'Yes, I realize that!' She pushed a hand distractedly through her long blonde hair. 'But, Andreas…I think she is the wrong choice,' she murmured. 'I'm sorry…I'm just getting really…really bad vibes from this—'

'Carrie, stop it!' He came across towards her then and caught hold of her arm. 'You'd feel like this about anyone right now…anyone who isn't Jo…or isn't you.'

She stared up at him and for a moment his dark face was blurred with her tears. Hastily she looked away from him, trying to pull herself together. He was right, of course; she didn't want anyone else looking after Lilly.

'OK…there is an element of that!' She admitted the fact huskily. 'But I still don't think that your choice is right.'

'My choice is exactly right.' His eyes held with hers. 'My choice is you, Carrie.'

Her heart flipped in a weird somersault of emotion. 'So…you really meant what you said last night?'

One dark eyebrow rose. 'I never say anything I don't mean.'

Silence seemed to swirl between them as she stared up at him.

'All you need to do is say yes to my proposal, and I will hand over the running of the house to you, and you can choose whoever and whatever help you want.'

She slanted her chin up firmly. 'I wouldn't need any help. I'd look after Lilly myself.'

He smiled. 'Shall I take that as a yes?'

Before she knew what she was doing she was nodding. 'Yes, Andreas.' She whispered the words huskily. 'I will marry you.'

CHAPTER TEN

THE sun was shimmering in a misty haze over the sea turning
it a milky blue. Even in the shade it was at least thirty degrees—
not that there was much shade. They were on board Andreas's
large ocean-going yacht, sailing across the liquid silk of the sea
towards the island of Mykonos.

Lilly was asleep in her carrycot below deck, a fan strategically placed to send cooling air over her. Carrie was at the
helm in charge of the wheel, watching as Andreas deftly
brought the sails down before walking sure-footedly over the
polished decks back towards her.

He was wearing shorts and a T-shirt and the casual attire
suited him; in fact she found she couldn't take her eyes off him.

This was the man she was going to marry in a short ceremony tomorrow.

Carrie still couldn't quite believe it. Since saying yes to him
ten days ago, the arrangements had been made with such
lightning speed that she felt slightly dazed, she'd barely had
time to extend her leave from work before she was swept
along with Andreas's plans for their wedding. Andreas had
suggested that they marry in Mykonos because it was where
his father lived and George Stillanos was too ill to make the
journey to Pyrena to attend. When Carrie had agreed she'd
thought they would set a date for a few months' time; instead
Andreas had coolly informed her when he'd arrived back

from work that Monday that the wedding was booked for later the next week.

It had been a very strange few days. First Jo and Theo's will had been read, a traumatic event in itself where Carrie and Andreas had sat side by side in a dusty solicitor's office to hear Andreas officially named as sole guardian for Lilly. But then that he and Carrie were named as joint trustees of a substantial inheritance that Lilly would receive on her eighteenth birthday.

Afterwards Andreas had taken Carrie to the graveyard to lay flowers.

Even thinking about it now made a shimmer of tears glaze her eyes. Andreas had placed a strong hand on her shoulder as they'd stood side by side at the graveside. It was the first time he had touched her since she'd agreed to marry him.

Even now as he joined her at the helm of the ship she was achingly aware of that fact.

And she wanted him so much.

'You can see Mykonos now on the horizon.' Andreas drew her attention to the land coming into view as he slid into the seat next to her.

She saw the arid hills rising steeply out of the sea, and as they drew closer the white sugar-cube houses that tumbled around the horseshoe harbour they were heading towards.

'It looks quaint, almost as if a child has drawn it,' Carrie remarked with a smile. And indeed from a distance the buildings were an enchanting white blaze against the rugged landscape, as if roughly drawn with a flowing brush.

'Yes, it's a beautiful place. An artist's paradise.' He turned the wheel smoothly, heading for the old port. 'The town is a tangled maze of winding streets. They say it was designed to confuse pirates.'

'Sounds intriguing.'

'It is. And as well as being exceptionally pretty it has some lovely designer boutiques. So if you want to go shopping for something to wear for tomorrow this is the place.'

Carrie shrugged. When Andreas had informed her he'd booked the ceremony for this week she'd nervously complained it was all too rushed, and that she didn't have anything to wear and he'd told her that what she wore was unimportant—that what mattered was their sincerity and commitment towards providing Lilly with a settled family environment.

And he was right, she told herself firmly now. Thinking about clothes and looking good was just a vanity—what did it matter? Andreas probably wouldn't notice what she wore anyway—he was only marrying her to give Lilly a mother. His only other interest in her was purely sexual. Probably the only thing he would notice was what she wore to bed.

The thought made her apprehension increase.

'As you said, it doesn't really matter about my clothes.' She shrugged. 'I have the suit I arrived in—the one I use for work. It will be adequate.'

'I didn't say it didn't matter what you wear.' His steady dark gaze met with hers. 'I said it was not the most important thing. But you should shop for something new this afternoon. I've organized a credit card for you. I'll give it to you once we are in port and you can have some fun with it, spend what you want.'

'Andreas, I have money of my own. I don't need to spend yours,' she told him tautly.

He slanted her a mocking look. 'You don't need to concern yourself about money. I am a very wealthy man—I can afford to buy you anything you want.'

'That's not really the point,' she told him hastily. 'I like to be independent. I always have been.'

'Well, now you don't have to be. Besides, from now on you will have an image to maintain—as my wife you will be expected to dress and look a certain way.'

Carrie glanced at him in alarm. 'You don't think the paparazzi will be snooping around taking photos of our wedding, do you?'

'As hardly anyone knows that we are getting married I

shouldn't think so.' He shrugged. 'Unless you informed people when you contacted your office to give in your notice.'

'Actually I haven't done that yet,' she admitted huskily.

'Why not? I thought we agreed that you would do that first thing Monday morning?'

She shrugged. 'Well, I've had other things on my mind.'

'Like finishing with the guy you were seeing?' he grated. 'You *have* done that?'

Why did that one little lie keep coming back to haunt her? she wondered furiously. She swept an unsteady hand through the length of her hair, wanting to tell him the truth—that the affair had ended ages ago. 'Andreas, I…' She trailed off for a moment, her nerve failing her as his eyes seemed to narrow on her. 'I already told you that Lilly is my priority, so, yes, of course the relationship with Mike is finished,' she murmured. 'We are getting married tomorrow, for heaven's sake!'

He was still looking at her with that intense, almost ruthless light in the darkness of his eyes. 'So why haven't you quit your job?'

'I will…my boss is away at the moment anyway. I'll speak to him the minute he gets back—actually I'm hoping I can still do some part-time work for them via the Internet. And he is the person who could sanction that for me.'

'I see.' Andreas shrugged. 'There's no need for you to work. But if it's what you want.'

'It is.' Carrie glanced away from him out over the sea. She didn't want to be totally financially dependent on Andreas. Her mother had relied on her father for everything and she had seen the devastating consequences of that at first hand.

'I can still hardly believe we are getting married tomorrow,' she murmured.

'You're not the only one. My father was stunned when I rang to tell him the news.'

'Probably given up on you settling down.'

'Maybe.' Andreas flicked her an amused look.

'Does he know that the marriage is merely for Lilly's sake?'

'No. My father's health hasn't been good for the last eight years since my mother's death. And losing Theo and Jo has placed even more strain on him. So I thought it best—all things considered—to let him think that this is a love match. Apart from anything else, he was so pleased that there was something happy to celebrate after all the traumatic events recently that I hadn't the heart to disillusion him.'

Carrie swallowed hard, the words bringing it home to her even more just how much of a sham this marriage was.

'I can understand that.' She tried to sound sensible and unemotional. 'And I'll do my best to play the part of dutiful, loving fiancée.'

'Will you now?' There was a teasing light in the darkness of his eyes now. 'Well, I look forward to that.'

She found herself blushing and he laughed. 'Which reminds me, I've bought you a ring.' He reached to the storage area beneath the ship's wheel and brought out a small square box. 'I hope you like it. If it's not to your taste we can exchange it here in town.'

Carrie took the box from him and opened it. An exquisite square cut diamond solitaire sparkled so fiercely in the sunlight it almost took her breath away.

'It's stunning,' she said, overwhelmed.

'I'm glad you like it.'

He watched as she took it from the box and then, before she could put it on, he reached and took hold of her hand, slipping it firmly into place himself.

The touch of his hand made her heart race.

'It seems like a good fit—I guessed your size well,' he murmured, checking how it sat on her.

'Yes—perfect.' She tried to keep her tone free from emotion, but it trembled slightly.

She looked up at him through the thickness of her lashes and as their eyes met she felt the sensual need inside her tighten painfully.

His fingers stroked across hers in a fleeting touch that promised so much pleasure and then he let her go.

'Now all you need is an outfit to wear tomorrow, and a trousseau to see you through a few days' honeymoon, and we will be ready.'

'A honeymoon!' Her heart flipped wildly like some creature that had suddenly decided to try and leap out from her chest.

'Well, I do believe that is the tradition—is it not?' He flicked her a roguish look. 'First the engagement, then the wedding where you promise to give yourself to me unreservedly, and then the honeymoon, where I take you at your word—is that not how it goes?'

He watched how her skin lit with even more colour, enjoying her discomfiture, enjoying teasing her.

'Well, as our relationship could hardly be classed as traditional, I rather thought we wouldn't be bothering with a honeymoon,' she murmured.

'Carrie…honey…we've waited this long for each other that I think a few days of uninterrupted sex is a complete necessity.'

She looked away from him, her heart and her body on fire with a strange kind of longing. She wanted a honeymoon— wanted to get closer to him, wanted to feel his arms around her, his lips possessing her—but she wanted it to mean more to him than just uninterrupted sex. She wanted him to feel the way she did… She wanted his heart as well as his body, *because she was in love with him.*

The simple truth hit her with the ferocity of a knockout punch.

She'd been in love with him since the first moment their eyes had met on that crushingly embarrassing first blind date when it had been so obvious he hadn't wanted to be there.

And when he'd asked her to stay on the island she had waited desperately for him to declare his love for her—but of course he hadn't and she had made herself walk away, had made excuses for her need for him, had told herself that her feelings were an illusion, that they couldn't possibly be real because she hardly knew him and what she had experienced had been nothing more than a holiday romance.

But it had meant more than that, much much more. She'd never got over Andreas. In fact she would go so far as to say that was why she hadn't been able to commit to Mike. Even when he'd been saying all the right things…she'd known deep down that her heart wasn't in the relationship.

And now here she was full circle with Andreas again—in love with him, wanting him and aching for him and knowing again that there was no chance of those feelings being returned. That he had only asked her to marry him for Lilly's sake.

Andreas watched the shadows flick through the beauty of her eyes and frowned. 'Carrie, if you've changed your mind and you don't want to go through with this marriage then say so now,' he told her huskily.

She felt her heart twist. She couldn't change her mind, she was in too deep, she realized in distress, and not just because of Lilly—although that did factor very strongly—but also because her heart was overwhelmed with her feelings for him.

She'd walked away once—but she didn't have the strength to do it again!

So she raised her chin defiantly. 'No, we've made an agreement, and I haven't changed my mind. I'm willing to give this a go—make a family for Lilly.'

Andreas regarded her steadily for a long moment, then he nodded. 'OK. I got the lawyers to draft up a contract for us anyway in case it doesn't work out.'

'A contract?' Carrie didn't think it was possible for the ache inside her to get any worse, but it did just then.

'Yes, it's just a standard pre-nuptial. But it also gives us the option to be able to unhook ourselves from each other relatively easily after five years if either of us isn't happy.'

'I see.' Carrie felt as if she wanted to cry; she could feel the wedge of emotion almost closing off her throat.

'My only stipulation if that happens is that you don't move

too far away,' he continued briskly. 'I'm sure you appreciate that we need to shield Lilly from any pain that a divorce would bring about and put her welfare above everything else. So you'll need to be somewhere nearby for her. I will of course provide a home for you and look after you financially—so you will have no worries on that score.'

Carrie tried to swallow her tears down. 'Seems like you've thought of everything…'

'Best to prepare for any eventuality.'

She nodded and wanted to say something flippant like, And what happens if I become pregnant…have you written that into the contract as well? But she didn't dare because her emotions were too close to the edge and it was all too raw.

'But hopefully it won't come to that. I want this marriage to work, Carrie, and I will do everything within my power to try and ensure that.'

He reached out and stroked her hair back from her face in an almost tender gesture that confused her senses.

'I want to make you happy.'

She tried to smile, but it was wobbly, and she felt relief when he turned away to concentrate on bringing the yacht into port. She mustn't cry in front of him, she told herself firmly. After all she was being ridiculous, it was a sensible precaution to talk about what was to happen if things went wrong. They had to consider what would happen to Lilly and how it would affect her. That little girl had been through enough losses in her life.

Turning her face up towards the sun, she tried to dismiss emotional thoughts and concentrate instead on the practical side of things. To be more like Andreas at this time, able to turn off her emotions on demand. She owed it to Lilly and to Jo and Theo to make this work.

'So if we are going on honeymoon what is going to happen to Lilly? Who is going to take care of her?' she asked quietly.

'Lilly is coming with us.'

'Really?' Carrie glanced back at him and smiled, touched

by the fact that he wasn't even contemplating leaving the child behind. 'Well, that's a relief. I know you said we need uninter-rupted…time together, but Lilly does need continuity of care right now…' She wished she hadn't started the conversation as she noticed the gleam in Andreas's eyes.

'Don't worry, Carrie, we will have that time together,' he assured her softly. 'I've made arrangements that will ensure Lilly's safety and we will have staff along with us. Plus don't forget that Lilly has long afternoon naps and we will have all the evenings.'

'I hadn't forgotten.' She looked away from him feeling dis-concerted. 'And my concern was for Lilly…nothing else.'

'Well, I hope I have reassured you,' he said wryly.

She felt far from reassured. Every time she thought of being alone on honeymoon with him her heart went into overdrive. She took some deep breaths of the warm salt air and tried to think of something else…anything else.

The harbour was quiet. A few fishermen shouted a greeting towards Andreas as he expertly tied them up alongside the quay and he answered them cheerfully. Then once the yacht was secured they strolled into the town. Lilly was awake now and Andreas carried her in a baby carrier that was strung around his shoulders. To the onlooker they probably looked like any ordinary family enjoying a day out together, Carrie thought as he waited whilst she admired some pictures on display in an art gallery.

'If you want to buy anything for the house, then go ahead,' he told her when she rejoined him a moment later. 'I want you to treat the house in Pyrena as your home.'

She flicked him a playful look. 'And just say you hate my taste?'

He smiled. 'I'm quite sure I won't.'

'But you might and then what would we do?'

'We'd compromise.' He reached and took hold of her hand. And she gave herself up to the pleasure of the moment, his possessive touch and the light-hearted conversation making her feel alive suddenly. OK, Andreas wasn't head over heels in love with her, but she could pretend. And maybe if they both tried really hard love would grow.

The thought spread warmth through her, dispelling the icy feelings from their previous conversations. She just wanted to forget all of that now, forget the contract he had talked so calmly about—forget the past and look forward to their life together.

The white blaze of the buildings with their colourful blue shutters hugged the narrow streets, curving around before opening up into a square where cafés were shaded beneath trellises of bright pink bougainvillea.

A few moments later they rounded another corner and Carrie could see tavernas lining the waterside and the iconic windmills of Mykonos.

Andreas glanced at his watch. 'We can jump into a taxi and go straight up to my father's house or we can sit and have a drink, and you can do a little shopping if you like?'

'The drink and the shopping sounds good.' She smiled shyly at him. She wanted this mood to continue between them, wanted to linger and enjoy the day.

A few hours later, after a relaxing drink of chilled Greek frappe, and some serious shopping, they took a taxi and headed out into the countryside.

Carrie stared out at the parched landscape sprinkled with the silver blaze of olive groves. They passed quiet coves and small villages before turning down a lane towards the farmhouse where Andreas's father lived. It was a traditional white house, the blue shutters and the tangled riot of creepers over the outside terraces giving it dramatic colour. But it was the view that took Carrie's breath away, because the house was perched by the side of the cliff, giving dramatic vistas down over the startlingly blue sea.

As soon as the taxi pulled to a halt by the front door Andreas's father came out to welcome them. He was older than Carrie had expected, probably about sixty-five, but still very good-looking, with silver grey hair and Andreas's dark penetrating eyes.

Carrie felt suddenly shy as Andreas turned from greeting his father to introduce her as his fiancée. She was debating whether or not to shake his hand, but found herself enveloped in a bearlike hug and kissed warmly on both cheeks, before the older man stepped back to look at her and said something in Greek to Andreas.

'Forgive me, Carrie,' he said instantly. 'I was forgetting you can't speak our language. It's lovely to meet you and welcome.'

'Thank you, George, it's lovely to meet you too.' She smiled, liking his friendly manner and the sincerity in his eyes.

'And I have to tell you that I was just remarking to my son that you are every bit as beautiful as he told me.'

Carrie flushed wildly at that, especially when she glanced over and found Andreas noting her reaction with an expression of amusement.

George moved to look again at his granddaughter, who was fast asleep in Andreas's arms. 'She has grown in these last few weeks since the funeral,' he said softly. And Carrie could see the look of grief and pain in his expression for a moment before he straightened and pulled himself together. 'Now come, let's go inside and relax and you can tell me all about your wedding plans.'

The inside of the house was cool and dark, the floors slightly uneven revealing the age of the building, the furnishings stylishly traditional and in keeping with the character and charm of the place.

They sat for a while in a lounge that had open windows all the way around allowing a soothing breeze from the sea to gently stir the air. George made them tea and they sipped it from china cups and talked about Lilly. The mood was relaxed and they found themselves talking about Theo and Jo and happy times from the past.

'I know they would both be so pleased about this wedding,' George reflected suddenly.

'Well, they did introduce us,' Andreas remembered with a laugh.

'Yes, and what an excruciating blind date that was!' Carrie smiled. 'In fact I was thinking about it this morning. Neither of us wanted to be there.'

'Well...I didn't want to be there until I saw you,' Andreas corrected her gently.

For a second their eyes met and held and Carrie could feel her heart thundering wildly against her chest, could feel the same tension swirling inside her as at that first meeting.

'Love at first sight,' George reflected softly. 'That was how it was with your mother and I, Andreas.'

'Indeed.' Andreas's gaze still held with Carrie's, impenetrable, unfathomable eyes that seemed to sear into her very soul.

She had fallen in love with him at first sight, she realized painfully. But for him...maybe at best it had been lust at first sight.

The thought brought back some of her earlier apprehensions, made shadows flick across the blue depths of her eyes before she glanced away from him towards the sleeping child in his arms.

'You know, I think I'll go upstairs and freshen up and change,' she murmured, suddenly wanting some space.

Carrie found herself directed to a bedroom upstairs at the back, with windows that overlooked the sea. There was a huge four-poster double bed that was draped in white gauze, probably as a practical measure to keep the mosquitoes out, but it looked impossibly romantic.

She wondered if Andreas would be sharing this bed with her tonight. Or if he would wait now until they were married... After all, the wedding was only tomorrow.

The thought made little tremors of nervous anticipation flutter through her. Trying not to think about it, she opened her overnight case and slipped out of her Bermuda shorts and T-shirt and into a more feminine top and skirt. Then she moved towards the window and tried not to think about the evening ahead, tried not to dwell on anything except the beauty of her surroundings. But it was difficult to tear her mind away from Andreas, especially as every time she moved her hand her ring flashed fire in the sunlight.

She remembered the feelings he had stirred inside her as he had slipped the ring firmly into place this morning, remembered how the lightest touch of his skin against hers had made her feel alive, had made fires of need flare furiously inside.

What would it be like to make love with him?

The question taunted her.

Unlike her he'd undoubtedly had plenty of lovers and would be very experienced.

And maybe she wouldn't measure up to his expectations…

The thought made her body tense. Maybe he would be disappointed that she was still a virgin, that she didn't know how to please him.

If he loved her it wouldn't matter so much, he would be content to take things slowly. But this wasn't a conventional type of marriage or relationship; there would be no words of love and the passion would be all-important.

She remembered the way Andreas had looked at her as his father talked of love at first sight. There had been no love in his eyes, just that sizzling sexual intensity that ate away at her.

Could she live up to that fire in his soul?

Maybe he would find her lack of expertise in the bedroom disappointing. Maybe after a while he would tire of her completely and eventually just take another lover. If there were no real emotions involved and it was just about sex, what was to stop him?

The thought struck ice-cold fear inside her. She didn't want that kind of marriage.

She'd always sworn that she would only marry someone who truly loved her, someone she felt safe and secure with. She didn't want to experience the heartache she had seen in her mother's life.

There was a tap at the bedroom door and as she turned Andreas came into the room.

'Is everything OK?' His eyes raked over her, noting the rigid tension in her body.

'Yes, of course.'

He looked at her with one dark eyebrow raised. 'You are almost as pale as the outside of the house.'

'Am I?' She smiled and tried to shrug away his concern. 'Maybe lying to your father about our feelings is harder than I thought.'

'Carrie, he's been through too much recently to be told the truth. He needs to avoid stress.' His voice was brusque. 'And anyway what is the point in telling him when we are going to try our best to make this arrangement work?'

'I understand. I'm just saying that it is difficult.'

He nodded. 'Don't worry, we will be leaving tomorrow straight after the wedding anyway.'

'Leaving?' She frowned. 'But I thought we were staying for a few days!'

'You think I want a honeymoon in my father's house?' Andreas looked briefly amused and she blushed.

'Well…' her gaze flicked to the bed '…it is a very lovely house.'

Andreas laughed. 'Yes, but we need privacy—and as I told you earlier we need some getting-to-know-each-other time.'

Code for uninterrupted sex, she remembered nervously, and her skin flared with even more heat.

'At least I am succeeding in bringing colour back to your face.' He smiled wryly.

'Yes—for some reason you seem to be able to do that very easily,' she muttered.

'And I find it quite fascinating.' He came closer. 'Sometimes I would swear you were still a virgin.'

'Andreas!' Her whole body was on fire now with embarrassment, but at the same time she was wondering if she should take this opportunity to tell him that he was right.

He laughed and the moment was lost. She couldn't tell

him—how could she? It was far too delicate and she couldn't bear it if he made fun of her.

'You know, you can sound so very prim when you want,' he murmured.

'Well, maybe that's just my personality!' She threw the words at him impulsively, wondering if perhaps she could use some acting skills to get away with not telling him at all. 'Maybe you will find me a complete prim disappointment when we finally go to bed together.'

He looked at her with a dark gleam in his eyes. 'I don't think so—somehow…'

She wished he wouldn't look at her like that; his expression was so composed, yet his eyes boldly seemed to almost undress her.

'I think I can hear Lilly crying.' Nervously she made the excuse and tried to step past him to escape, but he caught hold of her arm.

'Andreas, don't. I…I should go to her. She'll need her lunch.'

'She's happily ensconced in my father's arms. And although he tires easily these days he's quite capable of looking after her right now.'

'Even so…I should…' Her breathing trailed away as his head lowered towards hers.

'Even so…we have time for this…' he murmured.

'Andreas…' His whispered name was almost a plea on her lips, she wanted him to kiss her so much, yearned for him. But she was so scared by the feelings he stirred up inside her.

His lips covered hers with a hungry possessiveness that sent her emotions spinning. And before she realized what she was doing she was moving closer, kissing him back. It felt blissful, all the doubts seemed banished—all thoughts occupied by just one detail: how much she loved him.

She moaned slightly as, instead of increasing the pressure of the kiss, he pulled away. She looked up at him, her skin tingling, her lips swollen and parted.

'Believe me, you couldn't kiss like that if there was an ounce of primness in your soul.' He stroked a strand of her hair back from her face and for a moment their eyes held. 'And tomorrow night there will be no more holding back…no more pretence…'

CHAPTER ELEVEN

THE pale pink light of dawn was stealing over the landscape.

Carrie opened her eyes.

It was her wedding day.

She lay still, looking up at the drifts of white material over the canopy of the bed, watching how they fluttered as the breeze from the overhead fan caught them.

Was she really going to marry Andreas today? It all felt slightly unreal.

Her mind drifted back to last night. Some of Andreas and George's closest friends had called at the house to wish them well in their future together. There had been a party atmosphere. A veritable feast had appeared on the table, and ouzo and wine had flowed. Everyone had been so friendly—had all remarked on how much in love she and Andreas seemed to be.

Her eyes had caught with Andreas's across the table at one point and he had smiled that almost mocking smile of his.

Then at nine he had stood up from the table and had casually told her that he'd arranged to stay in town overnight.

'Last night of freedom,' someone jokingly said and Carrie tried to smile, but inside there was a cold swirling feeling of disquiet.

Andreas glanced over at Carrie and held out his hand to her. 'Apparently it's bad luck to see the bride on the morning of the wedding. So come outside and say goodnight to me,' he commanded with a smile.

Amidst a lot of cheering and clapping Carrie followed him.

She turned her face against the coolness of the pillow now, remembering the warmth of the night, the brightness of the stars and the moon.

The way Andreas had kissed her. Then laughingly ruffled her hair. 'Better make a good impression for the waiting crowd,' he murmured teasingly.

'So where will you stay tonight?' she asked.

'Why, Carrie, you almost sound as if you care.' He tipped her chin up to look deep into her eyes. 'All you need to worry about is being on time tomorrow. A car will come for you at eleven.'

Where had he stayed last night? The question tormented her now.

Lilly was waking up; she could hear her happily kicking her legs and babbling to herself in the travel cot that had been placed next to her bed. Carrie rolled over and watched the little girl.

Marrying Andreas was the right thing, she reassured herself fiercely. She couldn't let Lilly go, she loved her too much.

Trouble was she loved Andreas too much too. So much that the thought he might have spent last night with another woman was making her feel almost sick with jealousy.

She threw back the sheets and got out of bed. It was her wedding day—supposedly the happiest day of her life—and she wasn't going to spoil it with wild imaginings. She was going to trust Andreas, she told herself firmly, and she was going to give this relationship her best shot.

The morning flew by in a whirl of activity. Andreas had asked one of his friends to come in and help look after Lilly whilst Carrie got ready.

A hairdresser arrived to style her hair; a florist delivered a bouquet of roses…It seemed Andreas had thought of everything.

At ten forty-five Carrie stepped out of her room. The silk dress she'd bought yesterday looked stunning. It was off the shoulder and it skimmed over her slender curves emphasizing her tiny waist and billowed out in the warm sea breeze as she walked out onto the terrace where George was waiting for her with a glass of champagne.

'Carrie, you look so beautiful,' he said gently.

She smiled, touched by the genuine affection in his tone. And for a moment she thought with sadness about her own father who had abandoned her so cruelly all those years ago. She remembered sitting at the window in the foster home looking out for him, but he had never come. She remembered it had been Jo who had sat next to her and reached to take her hand.

'Thank you.' Her hand trembled now as she accepted the champagne from George.

'An emotional morning,' he reflected softly and she nodded, her eyes glazed with tears.

She wondered how Andreas was feeling right now and if he had any last minute doubts.

And from nowhere she found herself remembering that morning so long ago now when he had asked her to stay.

Remembered how he had mockingly told her he wasn't going to propose.

I can't offer you that kind of commitment—it's not who I am.

The words echoed inside her with raw emphasis.

Things had changed, she told herself firmly. They had Lilly to consider now and he did love Lilly. She had no doubts about that.

The sound of a car engine broke the silence of the morning and a white stretched limo rounded the corner and pulled up at the front of the house.

'Time to leave.' George smiled.

They brought Lilly with them in the car; she sat on her grandfather's knee looking adorable in a white dress embroidered with spring flowers. The hairdresser had secured a little band of yellow primroses in her hair and she looked so cute that Carrie felt like crying every time she looked at her because Jo would have been so proud of her little girl.

Andreas was waiting for her in the village square, standing nonchalantly in the shade outside a small white church. A few people gathered to watch as she got out of the car, but Carrie hardly noticed them; her whole attention was tuned to the man she was to marry.

He was wearing a dark grey suit with a silver waistcoat and a silver and grey tie. The formal clothing made him look even more formidably handsome.

She could hardly believe that this gorgeous man was soon to be her husband.

Andreas watched as she walked towards him, his gaze sweeping slowly and appraisingly over her, from her blonde hair so skilfully woven up and secured with tiny white seed-pearls to the way the dress skimmed her slender body so elegantly.

She smiled shyly as she approached his side. 'You look stunning,' he told her softly. 'Worth waiting for.'

He moved closer to kiss her cheek and for a moment she allowed herself to lean in against him, breathing him in, drawing strength from the moment.

'Are you ready?' he asked as he pulled back.

'As ready as I ever will be,' she whispered.

For a long moment their eyes just held. Then Andreas nodded and turned to speak to his father and to smile at Lilly before they proceeded into the church.

It was cool and dark inside, and it took a while for Carrie's eyes to adjust. There was a warm fragrance of incense and candle wax, mixed with the heady scent of the lilies that adorned the altar so majestically. As her vision became clearer she noted the surroundings were spectacularly grand for such a small church. Gold and silver ornamented the walls, and crystal and gold chandeliers hung from the high ceiling. Just a few friends from last night were waiting and Carrie smiled at them as she walked between the polished throne-like chairs that lined the small aisle.

Then there wasn't time to think about anything else except the ceremony.

When Andreas slipped the gold band onto her finger, he said something softly to her in Greek. Then he kissed her on both cheeks before claiming her lips in a light, yet infinitely sensual way that made her tremble inside.

A few minutes later and they were outside in the heat of the sunshine and she was cradling Lilly in her arms as everyone crowded around to congratulate her.

She'd done it—she'd married Andreas. The reality swirled inside her; she felt joyful, yet terrified. And those feelings intensified every time she so much as glanced at her tall, handsome husband who was now nonchalantly talking with the chauffer who had brought her here.

'I wish you deep and lasting happiness, Carrie.' George caught hold of her hand and smiled. 'And love as deep and as eternal as the love I still hold for my wife.'

'Thank you so much, George—for everything.'

At that moment Andreas appeared at her side and put an arm around her shoulder. 'The driver is waiting for us. We should go.'

'Where to?' She looked up at him with wide blue eyes.

'On our honeymoon, of course.' He reached to take Lilly from his father's arms, before shaking hands with the older man. 'See you next week.'

'I look forward to it…now off you go and enjoy yourself.'

'Oh, I intend to,' he murmured.

Carrie found herself blushing wildly as Andreas looked down into her eyes. Then he took her hand and they stepped away from the crowds towards the waiting limousine.

'I didn't realize we were going away directly after the ceremony,' Carrie said as they settled themselves into the comfortable leather seats and waved goodbye to the group of people waiting to see them off. 'I need to go back to the house to collect our belongings—'

'It's all taken care of. The bags are packed and back on board the yacht. We sail for Santorini in an hour.'

It was a wedding breakfast with a difference. They dropped anchor in the deep blue of the Aegean Sea and ate in the formal dining room that opened out onto the lower deck. The setting was exquisitely romantic, silverware and flowers on the polished table. No detail had been spared. There was chilled champagne and soft music and staff to wait on them.

It felt very decadent and the food was a delicious mix of Greek and Italian, all freshly prepared by a top chef who seemed to have turned the galley into a cordon-bleu establishment.

'This is amazing. I was so surprised when we got on board to find you'd organized all of this,' Carrie remarked as they were left alone again between courses. She was trying so hard to relax but she felt tense. Now that the ceremony was over and it was just the two of them, all she could think about was what would happen once the meal was over and the staff retreated, leaving them completely alone. 'Have you hired people especially for today or is this something you do regularly?'

She wondered if he realized how nervous she felt. Was she gabbling? Was she even making any coherent sense? Because sometimes when their eyes met she could hardly think straight.

Andreas on the other hand looked totally relaxed and composed. As soon as they had arrived he'd taken his jacket off, loosened his tie.

He smiled. 'I sometimes use the ship for corporate events and that's usually when I have a full complement of staff aboard.' He looked at her teasingly. 'But, no, this is not something I would do on a regular basis. I quite like being on board alone. I enjoy sailing—I find it therapeutic.'

'I know what you mean. There is something very tranquil about the water around here. It's almost glassy, it's so smooth.' She looked out over the sea. Even though they had been at anchor for a while she could still see the silver trail of disturbance they had left running through its satin surface.

'The conditions are usually good at this time of year.' He leaned back in his chair and his gaze moved slowly over her, noticing how creamy smooth her bare shoulders were against the soft material of her wedding dress. 'So now…have we more or less exhausted the small talk, do you think—or shall we discuss how blue the sky is too?'

The taunting question made her skin heat up. 'Am I boring you already?' she murmured, an edge of annoyance in her tone.

'Far from it—in fact you fascinate me, Carrie.' His voice was deep and somehow incredibly sexy. 'What you are doing is avoiding me—*already*. You could get a gold star in it.'

'I don't know what you mean.' She reached for her drink and tried to look unperturbed. But inside her heartbeats were increasing at a chaotic rate.

'I think you do—'

'So what would you like to talk about?' she cut across him, her eyes blazing almost as blue as the sky.

'Oh, I don't know, how about something other than the staff and the shipping forecast?' he suggested with a wry curve of his lips.

'OK. Why don't you tell me where you spent last night and with whom?' She tossed the question at him angrily.

He looked at her with a raised eyebrow.

'Don't want to talk about that?' she questioned. 'Well, I suppose I'm not surprised.' She tried to sound flippant but there was a dull pain in her tone that she couldn't quite hide.

'Carrie, I spent last night here on the yacht,' he answered her gently.

'Did you?' She shrugged. 'Well, it was your last night of freedom so it's none of my business anyway.'

'And I was alone.'

Her gaze slanted back to his warily.

'You don't have a very high opinion of men, do you?' he asked suddenly.

'Aren't you the guy who once more or less told me you just wanted me for sex?' She threw the question back at him furiously. 'So can you blame me?'

His eyes narrowed.

'Anyway, just forget it. Let's talk about the weather. Because really I don't care what you did last night.'

'Carrie, I—'

'No, really, just leave it.' She swallowed hard.

'I *was* on my own.' He reached for her hand. 'And I meant what I said about making this marriage work.'

The touch of his skin against hers made shivers of desire instantly race through her system. 'I should probably go and check on Lilly.' She tried to pull away from him but he wouldn't let her go.

'Lilly is fast asleep.' Andreas glanced at the security monitors on the sideboard that showed her sleeping peacefully in her cot below deck. 'Not only have we got sound, we've also got pictures.' He looked back at Carrie with an amused gleam in his eyes. 'So there's no excuse to leave abruptly in the middle of…anything—that's one of the reasons I thought it would be good to spend a few days on board.'

'Thought of everything, didn't you?'

She tried desperately to pull away but he wouldn't let her and then suddenly as their eyes met she didn't want to move away.

This was her husband.

She needed to trust him now…needed to put the past behind her for Lilly's sake and her own.

A member of staff came out to ask them if they were ready for their final course.

Carrie's breathing felt tight as her eyes still held with Andreas and she found herself shaking her head. 'Actually, no…I don't think that I could eat another thing.'

Andreas looked over and dismissed the waitress for the evening, thanking her for her time and asking her to convey his compliments to the chef for an enjoyable meal.

There was silence as they were left alone again…a silence that seemed to stretch and stretch into infinity as they just looked at each other across the table.

'What did you say to me today?' she asked him suddenly.

He frowned at her in puzzlement.

'When you slipped the wedding band on my finger you said something in Greek,' she explained.

'Ah…so I did.' He inclined his head.

'So?' She waited.

'I said that we are a family now. You and I and Lilly.'

She nodded.

'She was so good today, wasn't she? And she looked so gorgeous with the flowers in her hair…' Carrie trailed off. 'Am I not allowed to talk about that either?'

Andreas smiled. 'Lilly will always be a more than acceptable subject. And, yes, she did look very cute… Although I have to admit that I found it hard to drag my eyes away from you. You looked so beautiful you took my breath away when you stepped out of that car.'

She flicked a shy, uncertain look across at him. 'As conversation goes, that's very smooth. But thank you for the compliment.'

He laughed.

'What's so funny?' she asked with a frown.

'You. You sound so prim and polite.'

'First I sound like I'm…avoiding you and then…I sound prim!' Her eyes glimmered. 'What the hell do you want from me, Andreas?' she flared.

'*That.*' He stopped her with the single word. 'That heat is what I want—that fire in your eyes and in your soul that you like to try and pretend isn't there.'

'I'm not pretending—'

'Good. Because, as I told you, from now on there is no holding back.'

The sexual undertones in the comment weren't lost on her and she was acutely conscious of the way his eyes were moving over her, the velvet warmth in them almost caressing her.

His gaze lingered against the softness of her lips, his grip tightened on her hand and then he stood up, drawing her to her feet and around towards him.

'Now...let's start our conversation again...' He murmured the words softly as he lowered his head and claimed her lips with a passion that made her senses swim.

The kiss was slow and sexy and everything inside her instantly responded to it, her need for him flooding up inside with a tingling, forceful urgency.

'Shall we move this discussion to the bedroom?' he asked as he lifted his head. 'And you can tell me some more about how much you want me...'

She didn't even try to deny the fact, she was breathless and overwhelmed with so much longing that it would have been pointless anyway. Instead she nodded her head.

He smiled, a flicker of triumph in the darkness of his eyes as he led her by the hand from the dining room, down the stairs and the narrow corridor towards one of the cabins.

Carrie had never been down into this part of the ship before. It was cool and quiet, and the large room was stylishly decorated. A huge vase of orchids sat on the dressing table, champagne waited on ice by the double bed, silk covers folded back in silent invitation.

'Somebody has gone to a lot of trouble.' Carrie picked up the single red rose that had been left on the pillow.

'We've waited this long, we may as well have all the details perfect.'

But would the details be perfect? Nervous tension escalated inside her as they stood facing each other next to the bed. Would she live up to his expectations? And if she didn't...?

She swallowed the question down. It wasn't helping.

'Shall I help you out of that dress?'

She shook her head. 'No...it's OK...I can manage.'

His lips curved in an almost mocking way. 'Would you like a glass of champagne?'

'Yes...please.' She turned away towards the dressing table

and put the rose down before starting to take the clips from her hair. She didn't really want a drink, she'd left a glass untouched outside on the table, but it was a welcome distraction.

Andreas took his waistcoat off and his tie and put them down on the chair before sitting on the bed to uncork the bottle of champagne.

She flicked an apprehensive glance over at him. He looked casually relaxed, and so achingly handsome. The intensely white shirt seemed to emphasize his dramatic dark good looks somehow. He glanced up and caught her watching him and hurriedly she looked away again.

He smiled to himself as the cork popped and he poured them both a glass. Then he left hers on the bedside table and leaned back against the headboard to allow his gaze to drift over her.

Carrie tried to pretend that she wasn't aware that he was watching her, but her throat felt raw and dry with tension now. Maybe a drink was a good idea.

Her hair fell in a swirling silk curtain around her shoulders as she took out the last of the clips and Andreas felt something deep inside him tighten with pleasure. She was so utterly beautiful. He didn't know how he'd kept his hands off her these last few days. It had taken every ounce of will power he'd possessed, even down to trying to tire himself out physically by swimming long lengths in a very cold swimming pool morning and night. And even after that when he'd looked at her he'd still wanted her with a hunger that astounded him.

Watching now as she reached to unzip her dress, he felt the craving inside him grow stronger and stronger…but he forced himself to wait for her.

He wanted to watch her come to him with open invitation in her eyes. And he wanted to savour that moment…

Andreas had never made love to a woman who hadn't eagerly wanted him, and he was going to prove to Carrie that for all her pretence she *did* want him. He was going to give no quarter, allow no space for her to evade that reality.

Carrie struggled with one of the hooks at the back of the dress. 'Andreas?' She looked around at him after a moment. 'Sorry— I could use some help after all. Can you just unfasten me?'

'Sure.' He put his glass down and walked over to stand behind her. Carrie swept her hair over one shoulder out of his way and then closed her eyes as she felt his fingers brush against her naked skin. Deftly he unhooked the fastener and then slid the zip all the way down to her lower back.

'Thanks.' Her voice was husky and uneven. She was so acutely conscious of how close he was, she could smell the scent of his cologne, feel the heat of his breath against her shoulder.

For a second Andreas didn't move away. His gaze drifted over the vulnerable sensual line of her long neck and then down along the straightness of her spine. He wanted to draw her in against him, wanted to place his hands around that small waist, and kiss her delicate neck as his hands slowly moved upwards towards her breasts.

Instead he stepped back.

She hadn't realized just how much she had expected him to reach out for her and kiss her until just then.

'Andreas?' Her eyes flicked open and she swivelled towards him, her gaze wide and questioning.

'Yes?'

He seemed so cool, so calm…and yet her stomach had suddenly tied into complete knots of longing and distress.

'I…thought…' She stumbled awkwardly over the words, not knowing what she was saying, she was just aching so much for him to kiss her again…touch her again, and she didn't know how to communicate what she wanted. She felt tongue-tied and awkward and so needy that it was embarrassing.

His eyes swept over her flushed countenance, noting how she immediately tried to hide her eyes from his beneath the dark thickness of her long lashes, how she moistened her lips as his gaze touched them. Noticed how she had to hold her dress in place now to cover the naked curves of her body.

He reached out a hand and tipped her chin upwards, forcing her to meet the ruthless light of passion in his eyes.

And as her eyes slowly rose to meet his he felt a soaring exhilaration, because her need for him was clear and fiercely unequivocal.

His hand swept over the side of her face, caressing the softness of her skin, the silk of her hair, and she allowed the dress to slip through her fingers and slither to the floor.

CHAPTER TWELVE

'CARRIE, you are so exquisitely beautiful.'

Andreas's gaze travelled slowly down over her body, and the husky sensuality of his voice seemed to inflame her need for him even more.

She was only wearing a brief pair of lacy white pants that skimmed over her slender hips and some lace-top stockings that clung provocatively to her long legs. Her figure was shapely and perfect, her breasts high and firm.

His hands stroked down over her shoulders and her arms as he moved her closer in against him. His head lowered and then his lips captured hers in a possessive kiss that took her senses by storm.

She shuddered with pleasure as his hand circled her waist, drawing her in even closer and tighter against him. She could feel his arousal against her, and it made her breathing quicken with an almost dangerous need and excitement that was as old as time. Her breasts felt heavy and oversensitive as they pressed against the softness of his shirt, her nipples hard as they ached for his caresses.

With teasing light strokes he ran his hands down over her waist, his fingers stroking out over her smooth toned skin as he lifted her easily and carried her towards the bed as if she were light as a feather.

'God, I want you…' He whispered as he set her down against the silk covers. 'Want you so…so much…' He punctuated the words with kisses that trailed a heated blaze down the column of her neck to the pulse that was beating at the base of her throat.

Then his lips moved lower and lower, his hands tearing at the flimsy little pants she wore, stroking over her, finding the sensitive core of her, teasing her with gently provocative strokes that sent fires of ecstasy flaming through her.

Just when she thought she couldn't handle the pleasure that was building up inside her, he pulled away and started to unfasten his shirt. She looked up at him wild-eyed with desire as he started to unfasten the buckle of his belt.

His body was supple and muscular with not a spare inch of flesh.

Her eyes moved lovingly over the powerful lines of his chest and then down over the taut muscles of his stomach. Desire kicked like a mule deep inside her and she knelt up in the bed beside him, suddenly too impatient for him.

She smoothed her hands over his chest and reached to place a kiss on his lips.

For a moment she felt his body tense, then he kissed her back and this time all restraint was swept completely away as if a wild fire had suddenly taken over and was blazing out of control.

Carrie forgot everything except here and now and how much she loved him. She forgot to feel shy, to feel tense—she returned his kisses with a frenzied need she hadn't even known she possessed.

'Steady, sweetheart.' He pulled her back from him with a teasing smile. 'We need to slow the pace so that we can continue for longer.'

He watched the slow blush of colour flooding over her skin and laughed. 'Come here.'

Swiftly he pulled her further down in the bed, taking her over, using all his skills and his experience to pleasure her whilst maintaining control.

His mouth sought her breast, his tongue licking against the

hard aroused peak, his lips tasting her, his hands stroking her until she thought she would die of ecstasy.

'Now tell me how much you want me,' he taunted her as he straddled her, watching the way her eyes were almost cat-like, narrowed with blue-flame heat, noticing how swollen and hot her breasts were as they strained and begged for his hands and his lips to return.

'You know I want you,' she whispered. 'Please, Andreas, I don't want to wait any longer.'

He smiled and reached towards the bedside table. She thought he was reaching for contraceptives and caught hold of his hand. 'We don't need to use anything,' she whispered urgently. 'It's OK.'

For a moment their eyes met and his gaze darkened.

'Well…we are married…and I'm OK,' she amended impatiently.

He frowned and pulled back from her.

'I've been taking contraceptives because of women's problems…' She trailed off as his features relaxed and he smiled.

'Women's problems?'

'Andreas…stop questioning me. I need you and it's OK.' She reached up, and stroked her fingertips over the taut perfect abs, then lower still as she looked up at him playfully.

He said something to her in Greek, and the rich, attractive sensuality of his language combined with the perfection of his body made her feel as if she would just spontaneously combust if she couldn't have him right now.

He reached over again towards the bedside table and flicked the lamp on, dispelling the soft light of dusk that was stealing over the room.

Carrie was going to ask him to turn the lamp off again, but then he kissed her and she forgot about it.

He moved her legs further apart with his, firmly controlling where he wanted her. Then he possessed her lips again with a slow sensual kiss.

'Now where were we?' he murmured mischievously as he looked into her eyes.

'You were driving me out of my mind with passion,' she admitted huskily.

'Was I indeed?'

He caught hold of both of her wrists in one hand and brought them up behind her head, pinning her beneath him as his other hand slowly caressed the tautness of her up-tilted breasts.

Then suddenly he took her and the firm thrust of need made her gasp instinctively with pain and then with pleasure.

'Carrie?' He moved back from her immediately. 'Did I hurt you?'

'No.' She twisted her head away from him so that he couldn't look into her eyes.

'I did…didn't I?' He sounded puzzled for a moment. Then he said something under his breath in Greek and put a hand under her chin, forcing her to look up at him.

'Are you still a virgin?'

He watched the slow sweep of incriminating colour seep up under her skin and pulled further away from her.

'For heaven's sake, Andreas!' She looked over at him then, embarrassed and yet infuriated. 'Does it really matter whether I am a virgin or not?'

'Well, it obviously matters to you.' She was surprised by how gentle and patient his reply was. 'Carrie, you should have told me. I'd have taken care of you a little better.'

'I don't need you to take care of me!'

As he looked down at her Andreas felt a curious mix of emotions flood through him. He wanted to take care of her…he wanted to soothe her and hold her and make everything right…

'It isn't a big deal!' she told him, pulling the sheets around her naked body, her hair tumbling around her shoulders as she sat up, her skin flushed, her eyes vividly intense.

Andreas didn't think he would ever forget the picture she made at that moment.

'Well, it's a big deal to me,' he answered softly.

'Why…why on earth does it matter?'

'Maybe the more important question is why didn't you sleep with the guy in London if it's no big deal?' Even as he asked the question Andreas was fiercely glad that she hadn't. In fact he hadn't realized just how old-fashioned he was until this precise moment, hadn't realized just how much the thought of her with someone else had wrenched at his insides.

'I wasn't ready to sleep with him.' She shrugged and took a deep breath. 'And then he slept with someone else and… well, I found out about a month ago and the relationship fell apart.'

Andreas swore softly under his breath and pulled her closer. He had always suspected how vulnerable she was. He had learned from Jo how the past and the rejection of her father had affected her…made it hard for her to trust…and yet he was as bad as that guy who had hurt her in London, he reminded himself angrily. He'd chosen to ignore that over these last few days; he'd forced her into this marriage and into his bed.

Guilt tore at him.

'Andreas, you once told me that you would teach me about passion.' She looked up at him with wide blue eyes. 'And we agreed that we would try and make this work…for Lilly.' She swallowed hard. 'Have you changed your mind because of something so trivial?'

He smiled at that. 'It's not trivial Carrie,' he told her softly. 'And I haven't changed my mind.' No matter how guilty he felt right now, he didn't want to change his mind.

Relief surged through her as he drew her close and held her.

Then he kissed her again, deepening his exploration of her mouth, yet at the same time cradling her almost tenderly.

Her arms curved around his back, pressing him close as she arched her body against his. She felt as if she could never be close enough.

'I don't think you need many lessons where passion is concerned.' He whispered the words softly. 'But let's take it slowly from the top again…'

She laughed as he gently pressed her back against the softness of the pillows, relieved that he was willing to pick up where they had left off and that the awkward questions had stopped.

And this time Andreas took a more leisurely, languorous approach, teasing her with his hands, drawing her responses out, pleasuring her until she forgot everything except the wild need he was creating inside her.

She was almost ready to beg for him by the time he finally, gently, took her body. And this time there was no pain, just an incredible surge of pleasure.

Only when he was sure that she was ready did he thrust deeper and deeper, the gentle rhythm building with momentous intensity. Carrie had never known such sweet joy could exist, it was welling up inside her like a spring as he controlled her and matched her on each level with his own spiralling pleasure. Sensation built upon sensation as he whispered against her ear, forgetting himself and talking in Greek as he sensed her impending climax and only then allowed himself to lose control.

All-consuming pleasure exploded on wave after simmering wave of shuddering bliss.

Even after the explosion had occurred between them she could still feel the pleasurable aftershocks of sensation convulsing through her as he held her close and captured her lips with a sweet, searing kiss.

When he released his grip she went limp against him as if he had taken all of her strength, all of her energy; drowsily she buried her head against his shoulder.

'That was; oh; so good.' She whispered the words weakly and he laughed, a deep, gravelly laugh that vibrated from deep inside him.

He kissed the side of her face.

'And I'm suddenly so…tired…' She struggled to keep her eyes open.

'Then sleep, honey.' He drew her even closer.

'What about Lilly?' she murmured. 'She'll need her feed soon... Is she OK?' She moved her head to look at the monitor screen beside the table.

Andreas smiled and pressed a kiss against the top of her head. 'She's awake but contented.'

'I should go to her.' Carrie couldn't help it, her eyes were closing—the emotional day and the searing passion had taken their toll.

'I'll see to her,' Andreas said, his voice deep and reassuring. 'You sleep.'

When Carrie woke the cabin was in darkness and she was alone in the large double bed. Memories flooded back, of how gentle Andreas had been with her when he had discovered her innocence and how fabulous his lovemaking had been. Scorching heat invaded her body.

She had never known that she could feel like that. Andreas had shown her a side of herself that she hadn't even realized existed until now. Smiling to herself, she stretched out, feeling blissfully content.

Then, wondering how Lilly was, she sat up suddenly and looked towards the monitors. The cot was empty.

Andreas was probably giving the child her dinner. She got out of bed and went through to the en suite bathroom. There was a white towelling robe hanging up behind the door and she put it on and went back out into the corridor to check that all was well.

She heard Andreas before she saw him. He had Lilly sitting in her high chair and he was trying to interest her in a spoonful of food. 'Come on, sweetheart,' he said gently. 'It's good... you'll like it.'

He wasn't aware that she was there and Carrie stood in the doorway watching him for a moment, a smile on her face and an overwhelming ache of love in her heart.

He was wearing jeans and a shirt that was unfastened and

hanging open, and he looked gorgeous, powerfully sensual, all muscles and brawn and yet he was looking after the child with such gentle care that she found all her senses flooding with emotion, so much that she found she wanted him all over again.

She stepped further forward and Andreas looked around. 'Hello, sleepy-head.'

There was a sensual drawl about the way he said the words and it made her body respond very positively.

Aware of his scrutiny, she suddenly felt self-conscious about her appearance. The dressing gown was about three sizes too big for her and swamped her small frame and her blonde hair was silkily tousled and untidy around her face. Plus she wasn't wearing any make-up.

'How are you feeling?' he asked, his lips twisting in a wry smile.

'Fine.' She felt herself blushing and, trying to compose herself, she walked across to crouch down near Lilly. 'Hello, baby, how are you?'

Lilly gurgled happily and offered her a little teddy bear that she was holding.

'Thank you.' Carrie took it and then handed it back as Lilly reached for it again. 'So what's on the menu today?'

'Puréed parsnip stew, which doesn't seem to be a favourite.'

'You seem to be doing a good job of selling it.' She smiled over at him. 'You're going to make a very good dad.'

Andreas didn't return her smile. His mood suddenly seemed withdrawn or was it her imagination—was he just concentrating on Lilly?

'Anyway, as you are so busy I'll go and have a shower.' She felt slightly rebuffed for some reason.

'Yes, you go ahead.'

Carrie lingered beside them both for a moment. She wanted Andreas to reach for her and kiss her, but he didn't. And she didn't dare take the initiative, which seemed crazy after what had happened between them this afternoon. 'OK, see you later.'

She reached and kissed Lilly instead and then went back towards the cabin.

It was probably her imagination, she thought as she turned the shower on in the bathroom. Why would he suddenly be cool with her? Was it because she'd focused on Lilly, making no reference to what had transpired between them? Unless, now that he'd had her in bed, he wasn't that interested in her?

The thought swirled coldly in her mind as she stepped under the jet of heat and allowed the water to wash over her.

She'd been feeling all dreamy and happy—but just because they'd had a passionate time in bed didn't mean the relationship was a loving one. The knowledge kicked at her mockingly. Sometimes she could be so naïve—she'd made this mistake first time around with Andreas, thought that because he could kiss her with such fire and caress her with such tenderness he was falling in love with her. But he wasn't.

Carrie swallowed down the feelings of panic inside her. Andreas had never lied to her, never pretended he loved her. Nothing had changed and this was their first time together, she had to be patient—she shouldn't expect too much from him. Real love took time.

Anyway, maybe she was just imagining his coolness—she shouldn't be so sensitive. She snapped off the shower and reached for a towel. He was still grieving for his brother, for heaven's sake. Maybe when she'd mentioned about him being a good dad he had been thinking it should have been Theo that was there…Theo was Lilly's dad and always would be.

Carrie went outside and picked up her wedding dress from the floor and hung it up before unpacking her case and slipping into a pair of shorts and a T-shirt. She was sitting at the dressing table and had just finished drying her hair when Andreas stepped into the room.

'Is Lilly OK?'

'Yes, she's fine.' His gaze flicked over her. 'You look good.'

'Better than before.' She smiled.

He came to stand behind her and for a moment their eyes met in the reflection of the mirror.

'Carrie, we've been so busy we never got around to signing that contract I mentioned.'

She didn't know what she had expected him to say but it wasn't that!

'Contract?' She frowned and then her heart lurched. 'Oh, that…' She was going to make a flippant comment about not needing it now, but something in Andreas's eyes made her fall silent.

'Actually I have it here.' He opened up a drawer that was next to her and took out a sheaf of papers to place them on the dressing table. 'I've already signed it. You just need to.'

Her eyes locked on the pages, and she noted that he had put them down next to the rose that had been left on her pillow. The two things seemed to jeer at her, making her emotions simmer painfully.

'Take your time and read through it.' Andreas had moved back from her now and was casually buttoning up his shirt. 'But you'll find it is all in order.'

'Stating the terms and conditions of our marriage—no, sorry, of our divorce…' She could hear the bitter edge in her tone as she spoke and she desperately tried to clear it. After all she had her pride—she couldn't let him see how much this hurt. 'It's practical, I suppose.' She lifted her chin and made herself look over at him.

'It's for Lilly. As I said before, we have to protect her if this doesn't work out.'

He said the words so calmly, so matter-of-factly.

'Yes, I suppose we do.'

'Best to get it over with.' He found a pen sitting next to the phone and slid it across the table towards her.

'What—the marriage or the paperwork?' She tried to make a joke but it was a bad mistake because Andreas just considered her with cool reserve.

'Carrie, I've already told you that I want the marriage to work, but real life isn't always straightforward. We all have our needs—and our dreams—and if some time in the future ours don't…match…or meet up to expectations, then I don't want either of us to feel trapped. And we have that little girl out there to consider.'

'You don't need to remind me about that, Andreas!' Anger flooded through her. 'That little girl is the *only* reason I married you.'

For a moment the silence between them was loaded with tension.

Then he shrugged. 'I know we are both of the same mind.' His eyes were dark and intense. 'Lilly's well-being is the priority.'

Carrie bit down on her lip. She wished she hadn't just said that. Lilly was hugely important to her but…the words she had just flung at him weren't the complete truth… Somewhere along the way her emotions had become well and truly entangled in this.

'So read and sign the contract and let's just forget about it and move on,' Andreas told her coldly.

Carrie's heart was thundering against her chest. How could she forget how much she loved him?

She picked up the pen and without reading anything flicked to the back pages and scrawled her name.

'There.' She snapped the pen down and picked up her brush again. 'All done.'

'I'll leave it with you in case you want to read it later.'

'No need, I'll trust you.' Her eyes locked with his in their reflection in the mirror. 'Which seems to be something you have difficulty doing with me.' She couldn't resist the dig; it just slipped from her tongue.

'Stop it, Carrie.' His face was taut, his expression grim. 'You don't know what you are talking about. This isn't about trust. It's about being realistic and safeguarding Lilly for the future.'

She had been brushing her hair with long furious strokes,

but she put the brush down now with a clatter and swivelled around to look at him. 'How dare you speak down to me like that? You think I don't know that this marriage is a risk? Andreas, I have more reason to be sceptical and cynical about marriage than you—at least your parents were happy! My childhood was a shambles due to my parents' divorce.'

'Then you know how important this is.' He crouched down next to her. 'We can't allow something like that to happen to Lilly. And frankly—we are in uncharted waters...' his lips twisted wryly '...if you'll pardon the pun.'

She said nothing; she couldn't even raise a smile.

'Neither of us knows right now if we've done the right thing...only time will tell us that. So we will review things in five years—and be practical.'

Carrie knew he was talking sense, but his cold, almost clinical attitude was so hard to accept. She wanted to tell him that she knew now that she loved him...that she had loved him for the last two years and would still feel the same in five—wanted to tell him that no one had ever made her feel the way he did. She wanted to go into his arms and melt against him.

But he would just think she was being naïve. Because obviously he didn't feel the same way—if he did he couldn't talk like this, couldn't be so aloof and businesslike and matter-of-fact.

So she forced herself to shrug. 'You're right, of course. It's always best to be practical.'

He nodded and for a moment their eyes just held. 'I enjoyed this afternoon, by the way...'

The husky change of subject made her emotions seesaw wildly between desire and pain. 'Yes, it was...OK.'

'OK?' He looked at her quizzically. 'It was more than OK.'

His gaze rested on her lips and part of her longed for him to kiss her—the other part knew that if he did he might taste the salt of her tears, because she was holding onto her emotions with the greatest of difficulty.

She was very glad that Lilly chose that moment to make her

presence felt, her little cries of complaint echoing loudly around the room through the baby-listening device. 'I'll go and see to her,' she murmured, getting up hurriedly.

Andreas watched as she left the room. Then he reached and picked up the contract and for a moment his eyes fell on the rose she had placed there this afternoon.

He raked a hand through the darkness of his hair. The contract was necessary, he reminded himself fiercely. They had to know where they stood if things went wrong.

He was a realist…he had to be, for all of their sakes.

CHAPTER THIRTEEN

THERE was a full moon up in the sky. It shone a wide silver path across the calm surface of the water.

Carrie wondered where her path in life would lead… where this marriage would lead. Every time she thought about the scene in the cabin downstairs and that contract she wanted to cry and she hated herself for being so pathetic.

So Andreas had made her sign a contract—so what? He'd told her about it up front—it wasn't as if it were any surprise! She knew he didn't love her, for heaven's sake, knew this was no ordinary marriage. Obviously they needed to be practical—for Lilly. The fact that she had blanked out reality because of a fabulous afternoon of lovemaking was her problem.

She took a deep shuddering breath, the sensible words not really making her feel much better. Unrequited love was horrible—it could eat away at her soul if she let it. So she wasn't going to let it, she told herself angrily, hugging her knees closer to her body. Wasn't going to allow herself to dwell on it; she would match Andreas's mood. He was calm, cool and collected…and so would she be.

Except—how did he make love with such passion when there was absolutely no emotion in his soul?

The question tore at her and she hated herself for wasting time on it. It was a well-known fact that men were good at compartmentalizing. They could switch passion on and off like a light switch.

Carrie wished she could, wished it with all her heart because this hurt too much.

She heard a sound behind her on the deck and hurriedly she brushed a hand across her face to rid herself of any tears. She couldn't allow Andreas to know she was upset. It was too embarrassing—he'd think she was crazy.

'I wondered where you'd got to. Lilly has been sleeping for ages.'

Even the sound of his voice made every nerve ending inside her respond. 'I thought I'd get some air for a while.'

Andreas sat down next to her on the step and for a moment said nothing, just followed her gaze out through the rails towards the beauty of the sea. 'It's very peaceful out here, isn't it?' he reflected.

'Yes. Blissful.' She couldn't look at him. Her heart was still too full of feeling.

'After the last few weeks it's what we both need.'

'I suppose so.' Although he wasn't touching her and she wasn't looking at him, she was so aware of everything about him. The silk of his shirt against his toned muscular body, the dark gleam of his hair in the moonlight, the fact that he needed to shave and there was a slight shadow along the square jaw-line.

Even the clean male scent of him—soap…instead of the expensive cologne he sometimes used.

She breathed in the sea and the warmth of the night air and tried to close him out, but with every breath she knew she couldn't and that Andreas would always be a part of her—even if they went their own separate ways in five years' time, she would never lose this ache of knowledge from inside her.

Maybe she had enough love for all of them.

'Sorry if I was a bit emotional before.' She murmured the words softly.

'Were you?'

She flicked a glance at him and he smiled.

'Your timing asking me to sign that contract could possibly have been more subtle.' She continued briskly, 'Marrying someone for purely practical reasons is difficult for a girl to accept you know.'

'There would never have been a right time.'

'I suppose not.' She leaned back and looked up at the night sky. It was amazingly bright, the stars looked like flawless diamonds pressed against deepest velvet. 'The sky never looks like this in London.'

'Too much light pollution.'

'You're so…matter-of-fact.' She slanted another look at him. 'Tell me, have you ever been in love?'

He laughed. 'What kind of question is that to ask your husband on his honeymoon…hmm?'

'A stupid one, probably.' She shrugged. 'But we don't really know much about each other, do we? OK, we had ten days together two years ago…but we never really talked about…relationships.'

'Didn't we?' Andreas watched her, noticed how pale her skin was in the moonlight, how wide and bright her eyes were and how her hair looked like spun gold as it tumbled down around her back.

'Your father is a very romantic man,' Carrie reflected suddenly. 'He seems to have loved your mother very deeply.'

'Yes, so much so that he married her against his family's wishes—they eloped.'

Carrie looked over at him, fascinated. 'I didn't know this.'

'Caused a bit of a stir at the time. He was from a very wealthy family and worked in the family shipping business but when he went against their wishes they disinherited him. Theo and I grew up in the back streets of Athens. We had nothing.'

'That was harsh.'

'Yes, it was. But it was the kind of experience that makes you tougher. Makes you more determined.'

Carrie looked over at him. She remembered him telling her that he'd grown up in poverty, remembered at the time wondering if that poverty was what had driven him so hard with his own businesses. But she hadn't realized the background to the story…

'Then when my mother died my father got his inheritance,' Andreas continued. 'But by then he didn't want it. He gave it to us and we didn't want it either. Theo's is still in the bank— that's the money he has left for Lilly. And mine went to charity long ago. I used it as collateral to raise the money for the publishing firm, but I never touched it on principle.'

He looked over and met her gaze. 'Jo never told you any of this?'

Carrie shook her head.

'And in answer to your question, yes, I was in love once and I got engaged. But it was a long time ago now.'

Shock ricocheted through her. 'You were engaged!'

Her obvious astonishment amused him. 'Yes, I was. I suppose it was about five years ago.'

'So what happened?' she prompted when he made no attempt to continue.

'It just wasn't meant to be.'

He said the words so simply and yet there seemed to be a weight behind it.

Carrie's heart pumped hard against her chest. 'Let me guess—you put the business first and she didn't like it?'

'Something like that.'

He sounded resigned…or was that an undercurrent of desolation? She swallowed hard. It was crazy to feel jealous about something that had happened so long ago—but strangely she did. The fact that Andreas had loved someone else…and couldn't love her…hurt.

'Jo never told me…' She spoke almost to herself. 'Not that we talked about you much!' she added hastily. Which was true— both of them had skirted the subject of Andreas by tacit design.

'Actually Jo didn't know—neither did Theo. It happened when I was working in Paris.'

And it had hurt so much he hadn't been able to talk about it—even to his brother!

'So what about you?' he asked suddenly. 'And that Mike guy you were seeing in London? Were you very upset when you found out he was seeing someone else?'

She looked over at him—she couldn't tell him that next to him Mike had meant nothing! That he was the love of her life! For one thing her pride wouldn't allow it, and for another it would probably have him running for the hills.

For a brief second he saw a raw sadness in the beauty of her eyes. 'As you say, some things aren't meant to be.'

He reached out and traced a finger down over the side of her face. 'I know we've married for purely practical reasons, but we can make this work, Carrie.'

She nodded. 'I hope so.'

The touch of his hand against her skin was stirring up a hungry longing she didn't want to feel. He didn't love her, so for her pride's sake she shouldn't allow him to affect her like this. But she couldn't stop the feelings—it was as if her body was betraying her mind.

He leaned closer. 'And we are good together in bed…' he whispered the words softly. '…very compatible.'

'But it's just sex.' She forced herself to say the words. 'A chemical reaction in the brain—nature's way of saying we could make beautiful babies.'

Andreas pulled away and looked at her. 'I don't think so.'

She frowned at the coldness in his voice, but before she could say anything else he reached for her, pulling her closer. 'Let's just stick with the great sex theory shall we? I much prefer it.'

'Andreas—'

The pressure of his mouth against hers cut anything else she was going to say. And the kiss was no tender caress, it was ruthlessly and intensely demanding.

She found herself responding instinctively, winding her arms around his neck, and kissing him back. OK, this wasn't love, but it felt so…so good.

Carrie was staring dreamily out of the kitchen window. She was miles away. Thinking about the honeymoon. Pretending that all the emotions she had shared with Andreas had been real. It was a game that she had played a few times whilst they were away— and now they were home it was a method of relaxing that she was using more and more. It helped to allay the ache of sadness inside her—and she told herself that it was a harmless diversion.

She remembered the gentle rhythm of the days at sea, the bright pink of dawn, the scorching red of the sun as it sank slowly down beneath the horizon.

Santorini had been spectacular. One of the most dramatic of the Greek islands, its giant cliffs soared up out of the blue sea, and from a distance they had looked like snow-capped mountains. It was only when the ship had sailed closer that she had been able to see that the snow was really the picturesque white villages that stretched across its rolling heights. They'd walked along the narrow footpaths across the top of those cliffs, past the blue shuttered, whitewashed houses. Had stopped to admire the blue domes on the little white churches, and the sizzling blue of the sea. And they'd eaten lunch at a taverna perched on the dizzying heights of the cliff, with views that were so breathtaking that it had been like the set of some fabulous film.

All so beautiful it had been almost unreal.

But the surroundings had been real…and the food and the fact that she had loved almost every minute. The only thing that hadn't been real was the relationship itself.

Yes, Andreas had been passionate and attentive. But love had been the missing ingredient from the feast.

She kept telling herself that she couldn't have everything in life and that at least Andreas was making an effort to hide his lack of feelings—and that maybe one day he would grow to love her.

But they'd been married for almost three months now and increasingly it was a hope that her intelligence was telling her seemed less and less likely.

The days had fallen into routine. Every morning Andreas left early for work. Marcia arrived. Carrie gave Lilly her breakfast and spent some time playing with her. Then as soon as Lilly went down for her afternoon nap Carrie would turn on her computer and do some work for the bank.

She was just doing a few hours a week, helping to finish a project she had been working on before her departure to Pyrena. It was going quite well and it gave her a little financial independence, a need that Andreas didn't seem to understand since he'd given her a credit card, and her own account, but he'd gone along with it anyway.

In the late afternoons when the heat of the sun was starting to weaken she would take Lilly for a walk, then there was just time to bathe her and give her some supper before it was time to put her down again and wait with anticipation for the sound of Andreas arriving home.

However, this week there had been a new dimension to the routine.

This week every morning after Andreas left for work she had been violently sick.

Carrie filled the kettle and turned away from the window.

She couldn't be pregnant, she told herself reassuringly, because she was still taking the pill. She'd gone along to the doctor here in town and had got a repeat prescription. OK, there had been a slight delay getting her tablets; she had missed two days—but only two days…so surely the chances of conceiving were slim?

So whatever it was, she surely couldn't be pregnant?

She got out a cup and spooned some instant coffee into it.

Maybe it was a stomach bug.

The kettle boiled and she poured the water into the cup. The rich aroma of coffee filtered through the air, dark and heavy.

She lifted the cup to her lips, and tried to take a sip, but her stomach heaved so much that she had to hurriedly throw the contents of the cup down the sink and run the cold water. And still the scent lingered in the air, completely vilely nauseating.

She'd always liked the smell of coffee in the past.

Feeling weak, she moved to sit down at the table. Bang went the stomach bug theory. If it was a bug it wouldn't just strike when she had a cup of coffee… And it wouldn't be worse in the morning than at night.

She was going to have to stop lying to herself and get real.

No method of contraceptive was one hundred per cent safe…and when you missed a couple of tablets…

She could be expecting Andreas's baby. It was a very real possibility.

Carrie swept a hand unsteadily through her hair and tried very hard to think about this without emotion.

How would Andreas feel about them having a baby? Another baby, when Lilly was still so young?'

It wasn't something they had discussed. All their thoughts and all their plans had been focused firmly on Lilly.

She remembered joking with him on their honeymoon that their sexual attraction was just a chemical reaction—nature's way of saying they could make great babies. She remembered the way he'd dismissed the idea without even a smile, the way he had told her instantly that he preferred the theory that it was just great sex.

Then she thought about the contract they had signed, and Andreas's almost nonchalant suggestion that they review things in five years' time, go their separate ways if things weren't working out.

They weren't the words of someone who was even remotely considering the possibility of having a child with her.

Panic zinged through her bloodstream as she faced the truth. Of course Andreas wasn't thinking about making babies with her! People only planned things like that when they were in love.

And Andreas wasn't in love with her. He'd made that fact abundantly clear. He needed her to be a mother to Lilly and he enjoyed *making love* with her, but that was as far as his emotions went.

He'd probably be horrified if she told him that she was carrying his child.

The sound of footsteps on the stairs made Carrie try to pull herself together. Before trying to make coffee she'd been in the process of reading some spreadsheets that she'd printed out. The papers were sitting on the table and she pulled them towards her, trying to pretend that she was heavily immersed in them. She didn't want anyone to know about this yet—not until she'd had time to come to terms with it herself.

Marcia bustled into the room. She was doing laundry today and she had arms full of linen.

'I've just boiled the kettle,' Carrie told her cheerfully. 'You timed that very well.'

'Great. I'll just get rid of this washing.' Marcia was about to turn away and then looked at her again with a frown. 'You OK?'

'Yes, I'm fine.' Carrie forced herself to smile.

'You don't look fine…if you don't mind my saying so.'

'I think I'm just a bit tired.' Carrie got up from the table and went across to the sink to get a glass of water.

'Would you like me to make you a cup of tea?' the house-keeper asked, disappearing for a moment into the utility room.

'No, I think I'm going to stick to water today, thank you. It could be the caffeine that's making me tired.'

Carrie could hear the woman loading up the washing machine and slamming the door. A few minutes later she reappeared back in the kitchen and looked at Carrie with warm sympathy in her eyes. 'Is tea making you feel sick as well?'

Carrie could feel herself blushing from the roots of her hair to the tips of her toes. She hadn't said she was feeling sick!

'Caffeine used to do that to me when I was pregnant,' the woman continued briskly. 'It was horrible.'

Carrie didn't know what to say, she was so shocked that the woman had guessed, but then she supposed it was inevitable—Marcia did arrive every day at a time when Carrie was feeling particularly bad and she wasn't stupid.

'I'm not—' Carrie bit down on her lip, not wanting to lie to the woman. 'I mean I don't know if I'm pregnant or not,' she admitted huskily.

Marcia nodded. 'You need to go and see Dr Appelou.'

'I suppose.' Carrie swallowed hard.

'No suppose about it.' Marcia smiled. 'I'm so pleased for you both. A new life—new beginnings after so much sadness earlier this year—it's wonderful. Andreas will be so thrilled…' She trailed off as she saw the glitter of tears in Carrie's eyes.

'I'm not so sure he will be pleased,' she murmured, and it was a blessed relief to say the words out loud, to have someone to confide in.

'My dear, of course he will be pleased!' Marcia came over to her and pulled out a chair at the table to sit down with her. 'You two are made for each other.'

Carrie didn't say anything to that. She couldn't confide any further, couldn't tell the woman that the marriage was just a sham. It was too deeply personal.

'You know what the problem is, don't you?' Marcia reached and took hold of her hand. 'Your hormones are making you emotional, and that means you are definitely pregnant.'

Carrie smiled through her tears. She wished that her problems were as simple as that.

'It's the most wonderful joy to carry a child—you mustn't be frightened—and you have a loving a husband. What more can you ask…hmm?' The gentle words echoed inside Carrie painfully. 'You must tell him straight away—'

'I will tell him, but only when I know if it's definite,' Carrie said quickly.

'OK. But before that why don't you broach the subject? How is it you say…sound him out?' The older woman looked at her seriously. 'You'll find that he will be delighted. He loves children—he adores Lilly. It will be fine, Carrie.'

'OK.' Carrie smiled. 'Thanks, Marcia.'

Marcia nodded and got to her feet.

'Good job we haven't given those old baby clothes of Lilly's away yet,' she said with a smile. 'I'll put them in your room, Carrie—just in case it's a little girl.'

CHAPTER FOURTEEN

ANDREAS left work early. He hadn't been able to concentrate on anything today. All he could think about was Carrie.

She had looked very tired over these last few days. He didn't think she was sleeping properly and sometimes when he glanced over at her he caught a glimpse of such sadness in her eyes that it chilled him.

A curl of guilt stirred inside him.

He'd forced her into this marriage—had he put that look in her eyes?

The deeply unpleasant thought swirled inside him. He didn't want to face it because—damn it—*he needed her*! But the only time that she looked truly relaxed and happy these days was when she was with Lilly. Then the joy and the love that she had for the child came shining through.

For a second he remembered the way she had looked at him when he'd asked her to sign that marriage contract. The anger that had blazed in the beauty of her eyes as she'd told him that Lilly was the only reason she'd gone through with the ceremony.

And then later outside on deck how she had tried to put a brave face on things.

Marrying someone for purely practical reasons is difficult for a girl...you know.

From the controls of the helicopter he could see the island

of Pyrena shimmering below like a mother-of-pearl turtle in a deep turquoise bath.

It was a beautiful island but there wasn't much on it, just miles of white beaches and a few small hilltop villages. Maybe Carrie was bored; maybe he should suggest that they move to Athens. He'd only settled here originally because of Theo. He'd helped his brother to set up his diving business and he'd been more silent partner and financial backer than anything else. But he'd enjoyed getting involved and helping. The business was still running with the aid of a few loyal staff, but he didn't know what he should do about its future.

He brought the helicopter safely down and cut the engines. Then he reached for his briefcase and climbed out into the heat of the afternoon.

To his surprise he found that it was Marcia who was in the kitchen giving Lilly a bottle, not Carrie. 'Andreas, you're home early!' she exclaimed as he walked in.

'Yes, I thought I would surprise my wife, and catch a glimpse of Lilly before she's asleep for the night. For a change.' He went across and ruffled Lilly's curls and she reached her arms up towards him with pleasure. 'Where is Carrie?'

'Upstairs. I offered to look after Lilly and told her to go and lie down because she looked so tired. But you should wake her because I know she didn't want to sleep past three o'clock.'

'Thanks, Marcia.' He went out of the room and took the stairs two at a time, taking off his tie and his jacket as he strode purposefully towards the master bedroom. So he wasn't the only one who thought Carrie looked tired.

Maybe he needed to cut down on some hours at work, he told himself forcefully. He'd been behind with things because of all the time he'd taken off after Theo's death, and he'd even had to go in over the weekend last week, but he was catching up now and sorting things out. Perhaps Carrie needed him here more for support.

He opened the bedroom door. The curtains were drawn and

Carrie was lying on her side on top of the bedcovers. The room was in semi darkness, the overhead fan whirring over her. She was fast asleep.

Quietly he approached. She was only wearing the briefest of silk camisoles and a scanty pair of pants, and her blonde hair lay across the pillow like gold silk.

Something inside him tightened. She was so gorgeous, so sexy.

With a smile he sat down on the edge of the bed beside her and looked at her.

Her skin was so perfect and so translucently pale that there was an almost ethereal quality about it. Her eyelashes were long and dark and her soft lips were parted and a natural peachy pink.

His gaze moved lower to the soft, sweet curves of her body. He wanted her so much… The ravenous hunger that had been eating away at him all day as he dissected the moments of their marriage seemed to be unleashed like a sleeping tiger.

'Carrie.' He ran a finger up over her bare arm and across one creamy shoulder and her eyes flickered open. For a moment they were filled with a sleepy blue contentment as he caught her between dreams and reality.

'What time is it?' she murmured.

'Does it matter?' He leaned down and captured the softness of her lips in a sensually demanding kiss.

She rolled over onto her back, her arms moving up and around his shoulders.

'You are so delicious,' he murmured as he looked at her. 'So…very…very sexy…'

As he spoke he was sliding his hands up under the silk camisole, his fingers stroking over her taut skin, then he leaned down and kissed her lips again. 'And do you know that you taste of peppermint and honey?'

'Marcia made me some special tea.' She looked up at him from beneath dark lashes. Then suddenly she frowned and tried to sit up. 'What time is it?'

'Relax, it's only three in the afternoon. Marcia is looking after Lilly. I'm home early.'

'Three o'clock! I only meant to close my eyes for a few minutes!'

'You probably needed the rest. Do you feel any better?'

'I feel fine!' Her eyes narrowed for a moment. 'Why are you home early?'

He laughed. 'So I can see my wife and my little girl…in daylight hours. And I'm very glad I gave into the impulse now.'

'Andreas, I've got an appointment—I've slept in!'

'An appointment where?' He looked at her with lazy amusement in his dark eyes.

'With…' She trailed off. 'It doesn't matter…'

She couldn't tell him she had an appointment with the doctor, he would only start asking questions and she wasn't up to answering them.

'What is it—a hairdressing appointment or something? Do you want to ring and reschedule?' He leaned closer and kissed her again, his fingers sliding further up under the camisole, finding her breasts and stroking over them.

She responded instinctively to his touch, her breasts tightening with need. 'I'll do it later…' Her breathing quickened as she watched him unfastening the buttons on his shirt before moving towards his trousers.

'Take off the camisole,' he commanded huskily as he moved back to join her on the bed, unzipping his trousers.

She pulled the silk garment over her head and he watched the sleek gold waterfall of hair flowing around her shoulders, caressing her skin. His gaze moved lower to her breasts, so firm, so lusciously inviting.

Carrie leaned back against the pillows and looked up at him.

If only he loved her… If only this were real… The thoughts encroached, unwelcome and unwanted. She wanted to forget that reality because only when he held her, when he made love to her, could she feel truly close to him.

He saw the vulnerability in her eyes and it cut into him fiercely. 'Carrie…?'

'It's OK, just make love to me,' she whispered, reaching for him.

His lips crushed against hers, his body moulded against hers, his hands caressing her softly, slowly, tormenting her with needs that she couldn't resist, couldn't ignore.

He whispered to her in Greek, and she closed her eyes and pretended he was telling her he loved her.

Then he was inside her, fiercely claiming her completely. She arched against him, heat and desire escalating.

Usually Andreas took his time about pleasuring her, but today his pace was faster, forceful more demanding, no holding back, no tender kisses, compelling her to give more and more, taking her with dominant intention.

When at last she exploded in his arms he held her so tight, absorbing her shuddering sobs, her tiny gasps as his lips ravished hers.

For a long while they lay entwined and it was hard to know where her body ended and his began, they were as one…totally sated, totally exhausted.

He was the first to move. He stroked her hair back from her face so that he could look at her. 'Are you OK?'

She nodded, unable to find her voice. She wanted him to hold her some more; she wanted him to tell her he loved her…

He pulled away and she wanted to curl her arms around the manly power of his body, prevent him from leaving. But she didn't dare. It was so strange how she could feel so intensely close to him body and soul one moment and then oceans apart the next.

As he started to put his clothes back on she reached for her dressing gown on the chair and looked at the clock. If she didn't leave the house within the next twenty minutes she would miss her doctor's appointment.

'I'm going to have a quick shower,' she murmured.

He watched her walk away.

'Do you think you could phone a taxi for me?' She made the request just before she closed the door. 'I'm going to try and make that appointment.'

'I'll take you into town.'

'Thanks, but you may as well stay and look after Lilly as I know Marcia has to go soon. I was going to take Lilly with me, but there's no need now that you're here.'

'OK, that's not a problem. I'll enjoy some time with her.'

Carrie stepped into the shower and closed her eyes. She needed to escape to the doctor alone. She didn't want Andreas to know anything about a baby...not until she was certain there was one...

When she returned to the bedroom she was dressed in a blue summer dress that swirled around her slender body as she moved. Her hair was tied back from her face in a ponytail; she looked young and fresh and neatly groomed.

Andreas was talking in Greek to someone on his mobile, his voice crisp and businesslike, and his eyes followed her as she picked up her lipstick from the dressing table and applied a light gloss over her lips.

'Did you ring for a taxi for me?' she asked with a smile as he hung up.

'Yes, it should be here in a moment.' He moved towards the window to glance out and as he did so he saw the bag of baby clothes sitting by the wardrobe.

'Where did they come from?' he asked casually.

'I cleared them out from amongst Lilly's belongings. They are all too small for her now. They are newborn sizes and up to three months.' Carrie glanced at her watch. She really was cutting it fine for this appointment.

'I'll put them outside in the garage. We can donate them to charity.'

The firm tone made Carrie look over at him and there was a heartbeat of a pause. 'Unless we might need them...' she ventured, trying to keep her voice casual, but it wavered just slightly, her blue eyes locking with his dark gaze.

'We won't need them, Carrie.' His voice was determined and unequivocal. 'I'll get rid of them.'

There was silence between them for several moments. Carrie could feel a churning sensation inside her, as a deep longing for reassurance flooded through her body. He probably just meant they wouldn't need them because he'd want to buy everything new, she told herself fiercely.

'Well, we don't know that for sure…do we?' she asked cautiously. 'I mean…I might fall pregnant…'

He shook his head. 'Carrie, a baby is not on the agenda.'

It was only what she had expected, but the words were spoken with such quiet emphasis and so adamantly that they hit her like a physical blow. And it hurt… It hurt so much that she couldn't even answer him for a moment.

'Carrie?' He looked at her with a frown, noting how her eyes seemed to glisten like blue sapphires.

'I've got to go. I think my taxi is outside.'

She felt numb as she turned away from him towards the door.

Of course he didn't want a baby with her, she mocked herself as she hurried away down the staircase and out through the front door. All he wanted from her was sex and someone he could trust to look after Lilly. She was a convenience, nothing more.

As she slammed the door closed the taxi arrived. She couldn't resist glancing up at the bedroom window as she climbed into the back seat. Andreas was still standing where she had left him. He looked like a stone statue, rigid…unfeeling.

And she hated him in that moment…hated him and yet still loved him so much that she thought her heart would break.

What was she going to do if she found out she really was pregnant? Would Andreas insist on her having a termination?

The thought made pain lance through her and instinctively she put a protective hand over her stomach. She couldn't do that! She just couldn't! She would refuse—she would leave him!

But then what about Lilly?

She gave the driver the address for the doctor and then leaned her head back against the seat and tried to rest, tried not to think.

But closing off her thoughts was like trying to dam a raging river that had flooded its banks.

She kept remembering the heat of Andreas's lovemaking and then the cold way he had looked at her.

A baby is not on the agenda.

How dared he say that to her? She knew Andreas was a law unto himself—arrogant, dominant and he could say things that sometimes were totally insensitive—but she also knew the other side of him. She knew he was tender and gentle, and his love for Lilly was profoundly touching. He adored that child and was so protective…

And, OK, his feelings for her weren't deep, he didn't love her, but he had treated her with respect and kindness over these last few months, with passion and warmth. In fact there had been times when it had been frighteningly easy to convince herself that he did cherish her.

How could he say something so…sweeping…so cruel?

Anger and pain lashed inside her. She was his wife!

But he'd never pretended that theirs was a conventional marriage and there was a piece of paper in his office with an opt-out clause…

The memory stilled her thoughts.

It was all very well feeling angry with him, but maybe he was the one who was being sensible and responsible.

CHAPTER FIFTEEN

CARRIE was sitting alone at the waterside taverna looking out to sea. The sun was starting to go down in a misty ball of fire, setting the water alight.

She'd lost track of time since leaving the doctor's office. All she knew was she couldn't face Andreas right now, couldn't bear to see the look on his face when she gave him her news.

So she'd wandered down to the harbour and by strange co-incidence had found herself here, at the taverna where they had first met.

The place was practically deserted; a warm breeze fluttered the red and white checked tablecloths. One of the waiters was lighting some candles in preparation for the evening ahead. It had always been a popular venue for starry-eyed lovers, she remembered.

Her phone rang and she took it out of her handbag. It was Andreas. She stared at the name flashing on the screen and then put it back into her handbag again.

What was she going to tell him? She sounded out a few lines in her head. *Andreas, I'm two months pregnant, but you don't need to worry. I don't want anything from you. I'll move out...*

The phone went silent again.

But where would she go?

If Lilly weren't in the equation she would go back to London, but she couldn't leave the little girl—that would kill her. It would be hard enough to leave Andreas.

It looked as if they were going to have to resort to Andreas's Plan B, whatever that was. She wished now she had read the dratted contract when he'd told her to. She remembered he'd said something about living close by and sharing Lilly and that he would look after her financially.

Well, she didn't want his damn money, she thought furiously. She just wanted him to love her and the baby.

Her eyes glistened with sudden tears and, furious with herself, she looked out to sea.

'Are you waiting for someone?'

The familiar voice made her heart dip like a yo-yo and she looked up into Andreas's dark steady eyes with a feeling of incredulity.

Was she imagining this—could pregnancy make you hallucinate? Was this déjà vu?

She frowned. He didn't look like an illusion. He looked very real. His dark hair gleamed in the moonlight; his eyes were piercing as they held with hers. He was far too handsome. Always had been, probably always would be.

'I'd like to say that I'm waiting for some friends...' she shrugged '...but...'

'But unfortunately it's just me.' He pulled out the chair opposite. 'May I?' Although he asked the question politely enough, there was an edge in his voice and he sat down anyway before she could answer.

'What are you doing here, Andreas?'

'I was about to ask you the same question.'

'I'm having a drink.'

His gaze moved to the empty glass in front of her and he lifted a hand to summon the waiter, who came over immediately.

She listened as he placed his order in Greek and then looked at her questioningly. 'Do you want the same again?'

'I just want…' Her voice trailed off. 'I'm not in the mood for this, Andreas.'

He ignored her and finished placing the order anyway.

'I got you a glass of wine,' he told her as soon as the waiter left them.

'I was drinking carbonated water.'

'Since when have you drunk water?'

Since I got pregnant… The answer pounded inside her but she didn't say it. She couldn't say it because once the words were out that would be it. Game over.

'Who is looking after Lilly?' she asked instead.

'Marcia.'

'It's a bit late to have asked her to come out. She has her mother to look after!'

'Actually her mother is away at the moment visiting some friends. And when I rang her and told her that you had done a disappearing act she very kindly rallied.'

'I didn't do a disappearing act…I just…needed some space.'

He nodded and to her relief he didn't question her.

'How did you find me?'

He looked at her with a mocking glint in his dark eyes. 'It wasn't hard, believe me. There are only two streets in this town.'

'I could have been in another town.' She raised her chin.

'Yes, well, I took a guess you were at the nearest place… so…' he shrugged '…here I am. But it would have been helpful if you'd answered your phone.'

'I didn't feel like answering it.'

'You always were damn difficult.'

'And you always were impossible.'

Their eyes locked across the table.

The waiter brought their drinks and put the candle down between them.

Carrie wished he hadn't done that, she'd been happier in the twilight.

For a moment Andreas just watched her quietly.

'So have you come to any decisions?'

The question caused consternation to escalate. Did he already know? Had Marcia told him that she was pregnant? The thought made her heart start to thunder in her ears.

'What kind of decision are you talking about?'

For a moment there was silence.

'I think you know what kind of decision I'm talking about,' he replied curtly. 'The kind that involves staying within our marriage or walking away.'

Her breathing felt painful now.

'You know, Carrie, I'd thought that because we had Lilly that it would take longer to reach this particular crossroad.' His voice was bleak, his eyes grim as they held with hers.

He did know! She was shocked that Marcia had betrayed her confidence; somehow she really hadn't thought that she would.

'I think we made a mistake, Andreas. This marriage was never going to work…'

Her voice was husky and filled with pain. For a moment Andreas was transported back in time to another meeting just like this. Only it had been Francesca sitting opposite him, tears shining in her beautiful eyes as she told him she loved him but she couldn't marry him.

He'd thought back then that he couldn't feel any more anguish than he had felt that day…but he'd been wrong. It was magnified by a thousand times right now as he looked at Carrie. *Just as he had known it would.*

This was the situation he'd wanted to avoid when he'd pushed her away two years ago—in fact this was the situation that he had been so doggedly determined to circumvent that he had avoided all emotional commitment…ploughed all his time, all his energy into work. And it had been surprisingly easy to do that…until Carrie had come along.

But from the first time he had seen her sitting here, head tilted upwards, provocative blue eyes challenging him so fiercely, he'd fallen.

Somehow Carrie had got to him... Wheedled her way under his skin.

She stared at him now and he could see the emotion on her beautiful face, the glitter of tears in her eyes.

'Why don't you want to have a baby with me?'

She asked the question softly, so softly that the gentle breeze almost snatched it away from them.

'You think I *don't want* to have a child with you?' His voice didn't sound as if it belonged to him. 'Carrie, nothing could be further away from the truth.'

He reached and took hold of her hand. 'I want to have a baby with you more than anything else in this world.'

The gentle words made Carrie's heart turn over with joy. She stared at him. Maybe she really was hallucinating.

Yet the touch of his hand against hers was very real and it was sending warm, positive signals flooding through her.

'Carrie, I love you.'

For a moment her vision blurred with tears.

'I've loved you from the very first moment that I set eyes on you.'

There was a knot of emotion in her throat that felt as if it were going to choke her. 'Do you really mean this, Andreas? Because... I couldn't bear it if it was some kind of deception...'

'I mean it with every breath in my body.' His eyes didn't waver from hers. 'But I can't have a child with you.'

She pulled her hand away from his, her heart thumping viciously against her chest. 'How can you say that now after...? I don't understand...I—'

'Carrie, I'm infertile.'

The cool, raw words cut across the table between them.

She stared at him, saw the proud way he sat back in his chair now, saw the dark way his eyes had shuttered.

'I had mumps when I was younger.' There was a long silence between them for a moment. 'I never really thought about it much until I met someone when I was in Paris and fell in love with her.' He shrugged. 'She insisted she still loved me…but when it came down to marrying me…she had second thoughts…' He trailed away.

Carrie stared at him in bewilderment. 'Andreas, I—'

'So you see this is why I couldn't commit to you two years ago.' He cut across her firmly. 'But, when you returned to help look after Lilly I tried to convince myself that she would be enough for you—prayed she would be enough to hold us together. But deep down I knew it was selfish of me—that's why the contract was necessary. I knew this moment would come. I knew that one day I'd have to let you walk away.'

She suddenly remembered his cool words to her on the first night of their honeymoon.

We all have our needs—and our dreams—and if some time in the future ours don't…match…or meet up to expectations, then I don't want either of us to feel trapped.

Suddenly they made sense—suddenly everything made sense.

'Andreas, I'm not going to walk away from you.' She leaned forward. 'I love you.'

He shook his head as if he hadn't quite heard her and didn't believe her. 'Carrie…honey, I know you are hurting inside. I know you mean well, you married me for Lilly's sake, but—this isn't going away—already you are talking about children.' His voice was raw.

'I don't mean well.' She glared at him. 'And, yes, I married you for Lilly's sake. But I also married you because I love you, and I always will—with or without the baby.'

For a long while their eyes held across the table and then she reached for his hand.

'I mean it, Andreas. I have only ever loved you. There's never been anyone else in my heart.' She stood up from the table and went around towards him and slowly he rose to his feet.

'And can you just tell me again how you feel about me?' She whispered the question as she looked up into his eyes.

He took a deep breath. 'I love you, Carrie.' He stroked a hand along her face. 'I adore you. Worship you.' His lips twisted. 'Can't live without you...but that is selfish...'

'If that's selfish then I love you being selfish.'

He smiled as if he couldn't quite believe that. Then he lowered his head and he kissed her. It was such a searing, sweet kiss that it melted her inside and she clung to him, drinking him in, loving the feel of his body so close to hers.

A tear trickled down her face as he pulled back and she looked up at him. 'Andreas, do you believe in miracles?'

He smiled. 'Well, I met you...and you came back when I needed you most...so, yes... I suppose I do.'

Carrie looked away from him out across the empty restaurant. 'Let's get out of here. I've got something to tell you.'

He frowned, but left some money on the table and took her hand.

They walked silently along beside the water for a moment, and then she turned to face him.

'Andreas, I'm two months pregnant. I'm carrying your baby.' Her voice trembled slightly as she told him.

For a second he looked at her as if she were talking to him in some language that he didn't understand.

'We're having a baby.' She said the words again. 'I went to the doctor this afternoon and he confirmed it.'

Still he didn't speak.

'I couldn't believe it either—I mean, I've been using contraception and I only missed a couple of days.'

'Are you sure?' His eyes narrowed on her. 'Carrie, this can't be right. I don't want to dash your hopes...really I don't.' He reached out and stroked a strand of her hair back from her face with loving fingers. 'I would do anything to make this right for you, but—'

'There's no mistake, Andreas. I've seen the doctor. I'm definitely, *definitely* two months pregnant.'

'But all those tests I had...' Andreas frowned.

'Well…' she shrugged '…maybe we are just a very powerful, explosive combination. Or something.'

For a second he laughed. 'Of course we are. I've always told you that.' Then he shook his head. 'But—'

She placed a finger against his lips. 'You are going to be a father, Andreas.'

As her hand dropped back to her side she watched the powerful play of emotions across his handsome face. And then she folded into his arms and they just held each other.

Her arms swept up around his neck and he buried his face in against her neck.

'Some things are just meant to be,' she whispered softly.

'Like you and I.' He stroked a hand over her hair. 'You know I never want to let you go…don't you? *Ever.*' His voice was raw with emotion.

'I'm not going anywhere, believe me.' She smiled up at him. 'This is where I belong, here on this island with you and Lilly and our baby.'

EPILOGUE

THEY were both there when Lilly took her first wobbling steps and then sat down on the living-room floor. She looked up at them with a look of delight on her little face.

'Clever girl!' Carrie knelt beside her. 'Well done!' She looked around at Andreas. 'Did you see that?'

'Of course I saw!' He smiled.

For a second their eyes met and she knew that, like her, he was thinking about Theo and Jo and how much this moment would have meant to them too.

'I can't believe that she is toddling already!' Carrie whispered as she turned to kiss the little girl.

'I'm just glad it happened whilst I was home.' Andreas held out his arms to encourage the child to try again. And as they watched Lilly pulled herself up and headed towards him with a look of determination, her unsteady little legs moving faster the closer she got to him, until, gurgling with laughter, she flung herself into his arms.

They all laughed as he swung her up into the air. 'That is my clever girl,' he said softly, and the pride and love in his voice made Carrie's heart feel so full it was overflowing.

He glanced over at her and smiled.

'So you have no regrets about taking so much time off work, then?' She met his eyes mischievously. 'Not worrying about what's going on in that office—and whether you've delegated the right jobs to the right people?'

Andreas smiled. 'What office?'

'I never thought I'd see the day when you were this laid-back,' Carrie said softly.

'I never thought I would see this day either.' Andreas glanced down into the crib beside him where baby Nicholas Theodore George Stillanos slept so soundly.

His son.

Even the words sent a thrill of joy through him.

'Is he OK?' Carrie asked, going to stand beside him.

'He's more than OK, Carrie, he's perfect.' Andreas smiled at her. Then kissed her cheek…and then her lips… 'And I don't know why you would think I want to be anywhere else, but here with you.'

'Why indeed?' For a second she melted against him.

'However, there is one little bit of paperwork I need to sort out.' He pulled away from her and went across to the bureau in the corner and held up a sheaf of papers. 'I've been meaning to do this for a while—but frankly with all the excitement recently I forgot about it.'

'What is it?'

'Our contract,' he told her gently.

He noted how her eyes darkened. 'Andreas, I don't even want to think about that—'

'No, neither do I.' He cut across her quickly. 'But we have to think about it. The question is…should we burn it or shred it?'

As their eyes held she felt her heart turn over with relief. 'I think a celebratory bonfire might be a good idea,' she whispered huskily.

'I was thinking along the same lines. But just for good measure…' as she watched he put it into a machine at one side and pressed a button '…we'll shred it first.'

Carrie laughed. 'I never realized what a buzz it gives to be on top of the paperwork.'

'I know, it really is a great feeling.' He looked at the child in his arms and then with a smile he headed back to Carrie's side and put an arm around her shoulders to draw her close.

He still couldn't quite believe his good fortune; he had never thought that he would be so blessed as to have a beautiful son and this wonderful family. And every day he gave thanks for that—took nothing for granted. Jo and Theo had taught him that—had taught him that life was to be grabbed and lived to its fullest potential.

0609 Gen Std HB

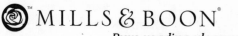

MILLS & BOON®
Pure reading pleasure

JULY 2009 HARDBACK TITLES

ROMANCE

Marchese's Forgotten Bride	Michelle Reid
The Brazilian Millionaire's Love-Child	Anne Mather
Powerful Greek, Unworldly Wife	Sarah Morgan
The Virgin Secretary's Impossible Boss	Carole Mortimer
Kyriakis's Innocent Mistress	Diana Hamilton
Rich, Ruthless and Secretly Royal	Robyn Donald
Spanish Aristocrat, Forced Bride	India Grey
Kept for Her Baby	Kate Walker
The Costanzo Baby Secret	Catherine Spencer
The Mediterranean's Wife by Contract	Kathryn Ross
Claimed: Secret Royal Son	Marion Lennox
Expecting Miracle Twins	Barbara Hannay
A Trip with the Tycoon	Nicola Marsh
Invitation to the Boss's Ball	Fiona Harper
Keeping Her Baby's Secret	Raye Morgan
Memo: The Billionaire's Proposal	Melissa McClone
Secret Sheikh, Secret Baby	Carol Marinelli
The Playboy Doctor's Surprise Proposal	Anne Fraser

HISTORICAL

The Piratical Miss Ravenhurst	Louise Allen
His Forbidden Liaison	Joanna Maitland
An Innocent Debutante in Hanover Square	Anne Herries

MEDICAL™

Pregnant Midwife: Father Needed	Fiona McArthur
His Baby Bombshell	Jessica Matthews
Found: A Mother for His Son	Dianne Drake
Hired: GP and Wife	Judy Campbell

0609 Gen Std LP

MILLS & BOON®
Pure reading pleasure™

JULY 2009 LARGE PRINT TITLES

ROMANCE

Captive At The Sicilian Billionaire's Command	Penny Jordan
The Greek's Million-Dollar Baby Bargain	Julia James
Bedded for the Spaniard's Pleasure	Carole Mortimer
At the Argentinean Billionaire's Bidding	India Grey
Italian Groom, Princess Bride	Rebecca Winters
Falling for her Convenient Husband	Jessica Steele
Cinderella's Wedding Wish	Jessica Hart
The Rebel Heir's Bride	Patricia Thayer

HISTORICAL

The Rake's Defiant Mistress	Mary Brendan
The Viscount Claims His Bride	Bronwyn Scott
The Major and the Country Miss	Dorothy Elbury

MEDICAL™

The Greek Doctor's New-Year Baby	Kate Hardy
The Heart Surgeon's Secret Child	Meredith Webber
The Midwife's Little Miracle	Fiona McArthur
The Single Dad's New-Year Bride	Amy Andrews
The Wife He's Been Waiting For	Dianne Drake
Posh Doc Claims His Bride	Anne Fraser

MILLS & BOON

AUGUST 2009 HARDBACK TITLES

ROMANCE

Desert Prince, Bride of Innocence	Lynne Graham
Raffaele: Taming His Tempestuous Virgin	Sandra Marton
The Italian Billionaire's Secretary Mistress	Sharon Kendrick
Bride, Bought and Paid For	Helen Bianchin
Hired for the Boss's Bedroom	Cathy Williams
The Christmas Love-Child	Jennie Lucas
Mistress to the Merciless Millionaire	Abby Green
Italian Boss, Proud Miss Prim	Susan Stephens
Proud Revenge, Passionate Wedlock	Janette Kenny
The Buenos Aires Marriage Deal	Maggie Cox
Betrothed: To the People's Prince	Marion Lennox
The Bridesmaid's Baby	Barbara Hannay
The Greek's Long-Lost Son	Rebecca Winters
His Housekeeper Bride	Melissa James
A Princess for Christmas	Shirley Jump
The Frenchman's Plain-Jane Project	Myrna Mackenzie
Italian Doctor, Dream Proposal	Margaret McDonagh
Marriage Reunited: Baby on the Way	Sharon Archer

HISTORICAL

The Brigadier's Daughter	Catherine March
The Wicked Baron	Sarah Mallory
His Runaway Maiden	June Francis

MEDICAL™

Wanted: A Father for her Twins	Emily Forbes
Bride on the Children's Ward	Lucy Clark
The Rebel of Penhally Bay	Caroline Anderson
Marrying the Playboy Doctor	Laura Iding

0709 Gen Std LP

MILLS & BOON

AUGUST 2009 LARGE PRINT TITLES

ROMANCE

The Spanish Billionaire's Pregnant Wife	Lynne Graham
The Italian's Ruthless Marriage Command	Helen Bianchin
The Brunelli Baby Bargain	Kim Lawrence
The French Tycoon's Pregnant Mistress	Abby Green
Diamond in the Rough	Diana Palmer
Secret Baby, Surprise Parents	Liz Fielding
The Rebel King	Melissa James
Nine-to-Five Bride	Jennie Adams

HISTORICAL

The Disgraceful Mr Ravenhurst	Louise Allen
The Duke's Cinderella Bride	Carole Mortimer
Impoverished Miss, Convenient Wife	Michelle Styles

MEDICAL™

Children's Doctor, Society Bride	Joanna Neil
The Heart Surgeon's Baby Surprise	Meredith Webber
A Wife for the Baby Doctor	Josie Metcalfe
The Royal Doctor's Bride	Jessica Matthews
Outback Doctor, English Bride	Leah Martyn
Surgeon Boss, Surprise Dad	Janice Lynn